DA[illegible]

Frederik Pohl was [illegible] New York in 1919. He started writing science fiction at the age of twelve and made his first sale at seventeen. As well as writing over sixty books, he has worked as an editor, a copywriter and a literary agent, and spends much of his time engaged in political and social concerns. His recent works of science fiction include *A Plague of Pythons* and *The Age of the Pussyfoot*.

DAY MILLION

FREDERIK POHL

UNABRIDGED

PAN BOOKS LTD : LONDON

First published in Great Britain 1971
by Victor Gollancz Ltd
This edition published 1973
by Pan Books Ltd,
33 Tothill Street, London SW1

ISBN 0 330 23606 7

Printed in Great Britain by
Richard Clay (The Chaucer Press), Ltd, Bungay, Suffolk

CONTENTS

INTRODUCTION

The stories in this book were written in odd places over a fairly long period of time, the oldest on a card table in Knickerbocker Village in New York around 1940, the newest begun in a hotel in Rio de Janeiro and finished a few weeks later at the airport in Nashville, Tennessee, waiting for a plane. They have really only two things in common. One is that they were written by 'myself' – I put it like that because I'm not really entirely sure that that twenty-year-old who banged out *It's A Young World* is much like the fifty-year-old who is telling you about it now. The other is that they are all 'science fiction'.

I put 'science fiction' in quotes because I'm not always sure what that is, either. 'Science fiction' is a poor name for a field of writing. It would be an uninspired one even if it were exact, and of course it is far from exact: there is a great deal of 'science fiction' that doesn't contain any science at all. (You will find some specimens herein.) But it is not entirely a misnomer, because just as 'science' is a state of mind and a systems approach to inquiry rather than test tubes and facts, so 'science fiction' is a *way* of writing stories. Harlow Shapley, talking of something else, once described this perspective as 'the view from a distant star'. It is a look at the human race and all its affairs from outside.

One of the most popular sports at science-fiction gatherings is defining science fiction: it is that kind of story which deals with events that may happen, but as far as we know haven't happened; it is that kind of story which takes some real event or trend and extrapolates it to its logical conclusions; it is that kind of story which would not exist if it were not for some central supposition which is based on scientific theory. Et cetera. I play this game as little as possible, because I am an inclusivist and try to avoid setting up barriers which might make me refrain from buying a story for a magazine or anthology I may be editing, or refrain from writing a story of my own, because it could be excluded by one of those barriers. But I do have a suggestion towards a definition, which seems to me attractive if only because it employs in defining science fiction that favourite writer's trick of standing a question on its head. It goes like this:

A science-fiction story is that story which might really occur anywhere in space or time, *except* that stories of our own real world are a special and less imaginative kind of science fiction.

In those terms, *Hamlet* and *War and Peace* and *Little Women* are examples only of a subclass within the general framework of SF. For reasons of vanity as a science-fiction writer, it gives me some pleasure to think that this is so. But vanity is not the only reason. Our world is but one of a very large number of planets – no one on Earth knows exactly how many there are, but a reasonably good guess puts it at sixty million or so – in our own galaxy, which in turn is but one of some hundreds of billions of galaxies in the universe. The events that Shakespeare and Tolstoi and Louisa May Alcott wrote about pertain to the history and customs of a certain kind of vertebrate, mammalian, carbon-based, two-sexed, air-breathing creature. We know a great deal about this species, and we can see how complex its societal and ecological systems are; but since they are the systems we move in, it is hard for us to see that they are the product of chance. Science fiction gives us the perspective that makes the job a little easier. Not always perfectly, in fact not always even very well, it does give us a look at our churches, politicians, addictions, morals, family relationships, vices and pleasures from the point of view of a frame of reference that takes none of them for granted.

When you think of how many millions of human beings have shot, stabbed, gassed, clubbed and burned other human beings because they thought *their* way of life was the uniquely best and proper one, it appears that this point of view could have saved us all a lot of heartburn over the centuries. It could save us some right now.

As I write, we are in the last days of the year in which human beings first walked on the surface on another world. It's only the Moon. It's really just our own back yard. There's not much there to want, and little enough of even that worth the cost of hauling back to Earth.

But it's a doorstep to the universe, and out there are many very wonderful things indeed, and to reach and master them we shall probably need all the wisdom and objectivity and freedom from parochial prejudice we can come by. We need them badly enough here on Earth, heaven knows, and if science fiction can help us attain these goals, it will have done more than a good many Messiahs.

FREDERIK POHL

Paget, Bermuda
December, 1969

DAY MILLION

On this day I want to tell you about, which will be about a thousand years from now, there was a boy, a girl and a love story.

Now although I haven't said much so far, none of it is true. The boy was not what you and I would normally think of as a boy, because he was a hundred and eighty-seven years old. Nor was the girl a girl, for other reasons; and the love story did not entail that sublimation of the urge to rape and concurrent postponement of the instinct to submit which we at present understand in such matters. You won't care much for this story if you don't grasp these facts at once. If, however, you will make the effort, you'll likely enough find it jam-packed, chockful and tiptop-crammed with laughter, tears and poignant sentiment which may, or may not, be worthwhile. The reason the girl was not a girl was that she was a boy.

How angrily you recoil from the page! You say, who the hell wants to read about a pair of queers? Calm yourself. Here are no hot-breathing secrets of perversion for the coterie trade. In fact, if you were to see this girl, you would not guess that she was in any sense a boy. Breasts, two; vagina, one. Hips, Callipygean; face, hairless; supra-orbital lobes, non-existent. You would term her female at once, although it is true that you might wonder just what species she was a female of, being confused by the tail, the silky pelt or the gill slits behind each ear.

Now you recoil again. Cripes, man, take my word for it. This is a sweet kid, and if you, as a normal male, spent as much as an hour in a room with her, you would bend heaven and earth to get her in the sack. Dora (we will call her that; her 'name' was omicron-Dibase seven-group-totter-oot S Doradus 5314, the last part of which is a colour specification corresponding to a shade of green) – Dora, I say, was feminine, charming and cute. I admit she doesn't sound that way. She was, as you might put it, a dancer. Her art involved qualities of intellection and expertise of a very high order, requiring both tremendous natural capacities and endless practice; it was performed in null-gravity and I can best describe it by saying that it was something like the performance of a contortionist and something like classical ballet, maybe resembling Danilova's dying swan. It was also pretty damned sexy. In a symbolic way, to be sure; but face it, most of the things we call 'sexy' are symbolic, you know, except perhaps an exhibitionist's open fly. On Day Million when Dora danced, the people who saw her panted; and you would too.

About this business of her being a boy. It didn't matter to her audiences that genetically she was male. It wouldn't matter to you, if you were among them, because you wouldn't know it – not unless you took a biopsy cutting of her flesh and put it under an electron-microscope to find the XY chromosome – and it didn't matter to them because they didn't care. Through techniques which are not only complex but haven't yet been discovered, these people were able to determine a great deal about the aptitudes and easements of babies quite a long time before they were born – at about the second horizon of cell-division, to be exact, when the segmenting egg is becoming a free blastocyst – and then they naturally helped those aptitudes along. Wouldn't we? If we find a child with an aptitude for music we give him a scholarship to Juilliard. If they found a child whose aptitudes were for being a woman, they made him one. As sex had long been dissociated from reproduction this was relatively easy to do and caused no trouble and no, or at least very little, comment.

How much is 'very little'? Oh, about as much as would be caused by our own tampering with Divine Will by filling a tooth. Less than would be caused by wearing a hearing aid.

Does it still sound awful? Then look closely at the next busty babe you meet and reflect that she may be a Dora, for adults who are genetically male but somatically female are far from unknown even in our own time. An accident of environment in the womb overwhelms the blueprints of heredity. The difference is that with us it happens only by accident and we don't know about it except rarely, after close study; whereas the people of Day Million did it often, on purpose, because they wanted to.

Well, that's enough to tell you about Dora. It would only confuse you to add that she was seven feet tall and smelled of peanut butter. Let us begin our story.

On Day Million Dora swam out of her house, entered a transportation tube, was sucked briskly to the surface in its flow of water and ejected in its plume of spray to an elastic platform in front of her – ah – call it her rehearsal hall. 'Oh, shit!' she cried in pretty confusion, reaching out to catch her balance and finding herself tumbled against a total stranger, whom we will call Don.

They met cute. Don was on his way to have his legs renewed. Love was the farthest thing from his mind; but when, absentmindedly taking a short cut across the landing platform for submarinites and finding himself drenched, he discovered his arms full of the loveliest girl he had ever seen, he knew at once they were meant for each other. 'Will you marry me?' he asked. She said softly, 'Wednesday,' and the promise was like a caress.

Don was tall, muscular, bronze and exciting. His name was no more Don than Dora's was Dora, but the personal part of it was Adonis in tribute to his vibrant maleness, and so we will call him Don for short. His personality colour-code, in Angstrom units, was 5290, or only a few degrees bluer than Dora's 5314, a measure of what they had intuitively discovered at first sight, that they possessed many affinities of taste and interest.

I despair of telling you exactly what it was that Don did for a living – I don't mean for the sake of making money, I mean for the sake of giving purpose and meaning to his life, to keep him from going off his nut with boredom – except to say that it involved a lot of travelling. He travelled in interstellar spaceships. In order to make a spaceship go really fast about thirty-one male and seven genetically female human beings had to do certain things, and Don was one of the thirty-one. Actually he contemplated options. This involved a lot of exposure to radiation flux – not so much from his own station in the propulsive system as in the spillover from the next stage, where a genetic female preferred selections and the subnuclear particles making the selections she preferred demolished themselves in a shower of quanta. Well, you don't give a rat's ass for that, but it meant that Don had to be clad at all times in a skin of light, resilient, extremely strong copper-coloured metal. I have already mentioned this, but you probably thought I meant he was sunburned.

More than that, he was a cybernetic man. Most of his ruder parts had been long since replaced with mechanisms of vastly more permanence and use. A cadmium centrifuge, not a heart, pumped his blood. His lungs moved only when he wanted to speak out loud, for a cascade of osmotic filters rebreathed oxygen out of his own wastes. In a way, he probably would have looked peculiar to a man from the twentieth century, with his glowing eyes and seven-fingered hands; but to himself, and of course to Dora, he looked mighty manly and grand. In the course of his voyages Don had circled Proxima Centauri, Procyon and the puzzling worlds of Mira Ceti; he had carried agricultural templates to the planets of Canopus and brought back warm, witty pets from the pale companion of Aldebaran. Blue-hot or red-cool, he had seen a thousand stars and their ten thousand planets. He had, in fact, been travelling the starlanes with only brief leaves on Earth for pushing two centuries. But you don't care about that, either. It is people that make stories, not the circumstances they find themselves in, and you want to hear about these two people. Well, they made it. The great thing they had for each other grew and flowered and burst into fruition on Wednesday, just as Dora had promised. They met at the encoding room, with a couple of well-wishing friends apiece to cheer them on, and while their identities were being taped and stored they smiled and whispered to each other and bore the jokes of their friends with blushing repartee. Then they exchanged their mathematical analogues and went away. Dora to her dwelling beneath the surface of the sea and Don to his ship.

It was an idyll, really. They lived happily ever after – or anyway, until they decided not to bother any more and died.

Of course, they never set eyes on each other again.

Oh, I can see you now, you eaters of charcoal-broiled steak, scratching an incipient bunion with one hand and holding this story with the other, while the stereo plays d'Indy or Monk. You don't believe a word of it, do you? Not for one minute. People wouldn't live like that, you say with an irritated and not amused grunt as you get up to put fresh ice in a stale drink.

And yet there's Dora, hurrying back through the flushing commuter pipes towards her underwater home (she prefers it there; has had herself somatically altered to breathe the stuff). If I tell you with what sweet fulfillment she fits the recorded analogue of Don into the symbol-manipulator, hooks herself in and turns herself on ... if I try to tell you any of that you will simply stare. Or glare; and grumble, what the hell kind of lovemaking is this? And yet I assure you, friend, I really do assure you that Dora's ecstasies are as creamy and passionate as any of James Bond's lady spies, and one hell of a lot more so than anything you are going to find in 'real life'. Go ahead, glare and grumble. Dora doesn't care. If she thinks of you at all, her thirty-times-great-great-grandfather, she thinks you're a pretty primordial sort of brute. You are. Why, Dora is farther removed from you than you are from the Australopithecines of five thousand centuries ago. You could not swim a second in the strong currents of her life. You don't think progress goes in a straight line, do you? Do you recognize that it is an ascending, accelerating, maybe even exponential curve? It takes Hell's own time to get started, but when it goes it goes like a bomb. And you, you Scotch-drinking steak-eater in your Relaxacizer chair, you've just barely lighted the primacord of the fuse. What is it now, the six or seven hundred thousandth day after Christ? Dora lives in Day Million. A thousand years from now. Her body fats are polyunsaturated, like Crisco. Her wastes are hemodialyzed out of her bloodstream while she sleeps – that means she doesn't have to go to the bathroom. On whim, to pass a slow half-hour, she can command more energy than the entire nation of Portugal can spend today, and use it to launch a weekend satellite or remould a crater on the Moon. She loves Don very much. She keeps his every gesture, mannerism, nuance, touch of hand, thrill of intercourse, passion of kiss stored in symbolic-mathematical form. And when she wants him, all she has to do is turn the machine on and she has him.

And Don, of course, has Dora. Adrift on a sponson city a few hundred yards over her head or orbiting Arcturus, fifty light-years away, Don has only to command his own symbol-manipulator to rescue Dora from the the ferrite files and bring her to life for him, and there she is; and rapturously, tirelessly they ball all night. Not in the flesh, of course; but then his flesh has been extensively altered and it wouldn't really be much fun. He doesn't need the flesh for pleasure. Genital organs feel nothing. Neither do hands, nor breasts, nor lips; they are only receptors, accepting and transmitting impulses. It is the brain that feels, it is the interpretation of those impulses that makes agony or orgasm; and Don's symbol-manipulator gives him the analogue of cuddling, the analogue of kissing, the analogue of wildest, most ardent hours with the eternal, exquisite and incorruptible analogue of Dora. Or Diane. Or sweet Rose, or laughing Alicia; for to be sure, they have each of them exchanged analogues before, and will again.

Balls, you say, it looks crazy to me. And you – with your

aftershave lotion and your little red car, pushing papers across a desk all day and chasing tail all night – tell me, just how the hell do you think you would look to Tiglath-Pileser, say, or Attila the Hun?

THE DEADLY MISSION OF P. SNODGRASS

THIS IS THE story of of Phineas Snodgrass, inventor. He built a time machine.

He built a time machine and in it he went back some two thousand years, to about the time of the birth of Christ. He made himself known to the Emperor Augustus, his lady Livia and other rich and powerful Romans of the day and, quickly making friends, secured their cooperation in bringing about a rapid transformation of Year One living habits. (He stole the idea from a science-fiction novel by L. Sprague de Camp, called *Lest Darkness Fall.*)

His time machine wasn't very big, but his heart was, so Snodgrass selected his cargo with the plan of providing the maximum immediate help for the world's people. The principal features of ancient Rome were dirt and disease, pain and death. Snodgrass decided to make the Roman world healthy and to keep its people alive through twentieth-century medicine. Everything else could take care of itself, once the human race was free of its terrible plagues and early deaths.

Snodgrass introduced penicillin and aureomycin and painless dentistry. He ground lenses for spectacles and explained the surgical techniques for removing cataracts. He taught anaesthesia and the germ theory of disease, and showed how to purify drinking water. He built Kleenex factories and taught the Romans to cover their mouths when they coughed. He demanded, and got, covers for the open Roman sewers, and he pioneered the practice of the balanced diet.

Snodgrass brought health to the ancient world, and kept his own health, too. He lived to more than a hundred years.

He died, in fact, in the year AD 100, a very contented man.

When Snodgrass arrived in Augustus' great palace on the Palatine Hill, there were some 250,000,000 human beings alive in the world. He persuaded the principate to share his blessings with all the world, benefiting not only the hundred million subjects of the Empire, but the other hundred millions in Asia and the tens of millions in Africa, the Western Hemisphere and all the Pacific islands.

Everybody got healthy.

Infant mortality dropped at once, from ninety deaths in a hundred to fewer than two. Life expectancies doubled immediately. Everyone was well, and demonstrated their health by having more children, who grew in health to maturity and had more.

It is a feeble population that cannot double itself every generation if it tries.

These Romans, Goths and Mongols were tough. Every thirty years the population of the world increased by a factor of two. In the year AD 30, the world population was a half-billion. In AD 60, it was a full billion. By the time Snodgrass passed away, a happy man, it was as large as it is today.

It is too bad that Snodgrass did not have room in his time machine for the blueprints of cargo ships, the texts on metallurgy to build the tools that would make the reapers that would harvest the fields – for the triple-expansion steam turbines that would generate the electricity that would power the machines that would run the cities – for all the technology that two thousand subsequent years had brought about.

But he didn't.

Consequently by the time of his death conditions were no longer quite perfect. A great many were badly housed.

On the whole, Snodgrass was pleased, for all these things could surely take care of themselves. With a healthy world population, the increase of numbers would be a mere spur to research. Boundless nature, once its ways were studied, would surely provide for any number of human beings.

Indeed it did. Steam engines on the Newcomen design were lifting water to irrigate fields to grow food long before his death. The Nile was dammed at Aswan in the year 55. Battery-powered street cars replaced oxcarts in Rome and Alexandria before AD 75, and the galley slaves were freed by huge, clumsy diesel outboards that drove the food ships across the Mediterranean a few years later.

In the year AD 200 the world had now something over twenty billion souls, and technology was running neck-and-neck with expansion. Nuclear-driven ploughs had cleared the Teutoburg Wald, where Varus' bones were still mouldering, and fertilizer made from ion-exchange mining of the sea produced fantastic crops of hybrid grains. In AD 300 the world population stood at a quarter of a trillion. Hydrogen fusion produced fabulous quantities of energy from the sea; atomic transmutation converted any matter into food. This was necessary, because there was no longer any room for farms. The Earth was getting crowded. By the middle of the sixth century the 60,000,000 square miles of land surface on the Earth was so well covered that no human being standing anywhere on dry land could stretch out his arms in any direction without touching another human being standing beside him.

But everyone was healthy, and science marched on. The seas were drained, which immediately tripled the available land area. (In fifty years the sea bottoms were also full.) Energy which had come from the fusion of marine hydrogen now came by the tapping of the full energy output of the Sun, through gigantic 'mirrors' composed of pure force. The other planets froze, of course; but this no longer mattered, since in the decades that followed they were disintegrated for the sake of the energy at their cores. So was the Sun. Maintaining life on Earth on such artificial standards was prodigal of energy consumption; in time every star in the Galaxy was transmitting its total power output to the Earth, and plans were afoot to tap Andromeda, which would care for all necessary expansion for – thirty years.

At this point a calculation was made.

Taking the weight of the average man at about a hundred and thirty pounds – in round numbers, 6 x 10^4 grammes – and allowing for a continued doubling of population every thirty years (although there was no such thing as a 'year' any more, since the Sun had been disintegrated; now a lonely Earth floated aimlessly towards Vega), it was discovered that by the year 1970 the total mass of human flesh, bone and blood would be 6 x 10^{27} grammes.

This presented a problem. The total mass of the Earth itself was only 5·98 x 10^{27} grammes. Already humanity lived in burrows penetrating crust and basalt and quarrying into the congealed nickel-iron core; by 1970 all the core itself would have been transmuted into living men and women, and their galleries would have to be tunnelled through masses of their own bodies, a writhing, squeezed ball of living corpses drifting through space.

Moreover simple arithmetic showed that this was not the end. In finite time the mass of human beings would equal the total mass of the Galaxy; and in some further time it would equal and exceed the total mass of *all* galaxies everywhere.

This state of affairs could no longer be tolerated, and so a project was launched.

With some difficulty resources were diverted to permit the construction of a small but important device. It was a time machine. With one volunteer aboard (selected from the nine hundred trillion who applied) it went back to the year 1. It's cargo was only a hunting rifle with one cartridge, and with that cartridge the volunteer assassinated Snodgrass as he trudged up the Palatine.

To the great (if only potential) joy of some quintillions of never-to-be-born persons, Darkness blessedly fell.

THE DAY THE MARTIANS CAME

THERE WERE TWO cots in every room of the motel, besides the usual number of beds, and Mr Mandala, the manager, had converted the rear section of the lobby into a men's dormitory. Nevertheless he was not satisfied and was trying to persuade his coloured bellmen to clean out the trunk room and put cots in that too. 'Now, please, Mr Mandala,' the bell captain said, speaking loudly over the noise in the lounge, 'you know we'd do it for you if we could. But it cannot be, because first we don't have any other place to put those old TV sets you want to save and because second we don't *have* any more cots.'

'You're arguing with me, Ernest. I told you to quit arguing with me,' said Mr Mandala. He drummed his fingers on the registration desk and looked angrily around the lobby. There were at least forty people in it, talking, playing cards and dozing. The television set was mumbling away in a recap of the NASA releases, and on the screen Mr Mandala could see a picture of one of the Martians, gazing into the camera and weeping large, gelatinous tears.

'Quit that,' ordered Mr Mandala, turning in time to catch his bellmen looking at the screen. 'I don't pay you to watch TV. Go see if you can help out in the kitchen.'

'We been in the kitchen, Mr Mandala. They don't need us.'

'Go when I tell you to go, Ernest! You too, Berzie.' He watched them go through the service hall and wished he could get rid of some of the crowd in the lounge as easily. They filled every seat and the overflow sat on the arms of the chairs, leaned against the walls and filled the booths in the bar, which had been closed for the past two hours because of the law. According to the registration slips they were nearly all from newspapers, wire services, radio and television networks and so on, waiting to go to the morning briefing at Cape Kennedy. Mr Mandala wished morning would come. He didn't like so many of them cluttering up his lounge, especially since he was pretty sure a lot of them were not even registered guests.

On the television screen a hastily edited tape was now showing the return of the Algonquin Nine space probe to Mars but no one was watching it. It was the third time that particular tape had been repeated since midnight and everybody had seen it at least once; but when it changed to another shot of one of the Martians, looking like a sad dachshund with elongated seal-flippers for limbs, one of the poker players stirred and cried: 'I got a Martian joke! Why doesn't a Martian swim in the Atlantic Ocean?'

'It's your bet,' said the dealer.

'Because he'd leave a ring around it,' said the reporter, folding his cards. No one laughed, not even Mr Mandala, although some of the jokes had been pretty good. Everybody was beginning to get tired of them, or perhaps just tired.

Mr Mandala had missed the first excitement about the Martians, because he had been asleep. When the day manager phoned him waking him up, Mr Mandala had thought, first, that it was a joke and, secondly, that the day man was out of his mind; after all, who would care if the Mars probe had come back with some kind of animals? Or even if they weren't animals, exactly. When he found out how many reservations were coming in over the teletype he realized that some people did in fact care. However, Mr Mandala didn't take much interest in things like that. It was nice the Martians had come, since they had filled his motel, and every other motel within a hundred miles of Cape Kennedy, but when you had said that you had said everything about the Martians that mattered to Mr Mandala.

On the television screen the picture went to black and was

replaced by the legend *Bulletin from NBC News*. The poker game paused momentarily.

The lounge was almost quiet as an invisible announcer read a new release from NASA: 'Dr Hugo Bache, the Fort Worth, Texas, veterinarian who arrived late this evening to examine the Martians at the Patrick Air Force Base reception centre, has issued a preliminary report which has just been released by Colonel Eric T. "Happy" Wingerter, speaking for the National Aeronautics and Space Administration.'

A wire-service man yelled, 'Turn it up!' There was a convulsive movement around the set. The sound vanished entirely for a moment, then blasted out:

'... Martians are vertebrate, warm-blooded and apparently mammalian. A superficial examination indicates a generally low level of metabolism, although Dr Bache states that it is possible that this is in some measure the result of their difficult and confined voyage through 137,000,000 miles of space in the specimen chamber of the Algonquin Nine spacecraft. There is no, repeat no, evidence of communicable disease, although standing sterilization precautions are...'

'Hell he says,' cried somebody, probably a stringer from CBS. 'Walter Cronkite had an interview with the Mayo Clinic that...'

'Shut up!' bellowed a dozen voices, and the TV became audible again:

'...completes the full text of the report from Dr Hugo Bache as released at this hour by Colonel "Happy" Wingerter.' There was a pause; then the announcer's voice, weary but game, found its place and went on with a recap of the previous half-dozen stories. The poker game began again as the announcer was describing the news conference with Dr Sam Sullivan of the Linguistic Institute of the University of Indiana, and his conclusions that the sounds made by the Martians were indeed some sort of a language.

What nonsense, thought Mr Mandala, drugged and drowsy. He pulled a stool over and sat down, half asleep.

Then the noise of laughter woke him and he straightened up belligerently. He tapped his call bell for attention. 'Gentlemen! Ladies! Please!' he cried. 'It's four o'clock in the morning. Our other guests are trying to sleep.'

'Yeah, sure,' said the CBS man, holding up one hand impatiently, 'but wait a minute. I got one. What's a Martian high-rise? You give up?'

'Go ahead,' said a red-haired girl, a staffer from *Life*.

'Twenty-seven floors of basement apartments!'

The girl said, 'All right, I got one too. What is a Martian female's religious injunction requiring her to keep her eyes closed during intercourse?' She waited a beat. 'God forbid she should see her husband have a good time!'

'Are we playing poker or not?' groaned one of the players, but they were too many for him. 'Who won the Martian beauty contest? ... Nobody won! How do you get a Martian female to give up sex? ... Marry her!' Mr Mandala laughed out loud at that one, and when one of the reporters came to him and asked for a book of matches he gave it to him. 'Ta,' said the man, puffing his pipe alight. 'Long night, eh?'

'You bet,' said Mr Mandala genially. On the television screen the tape was running again, for the fourth time. Mr Mandala yawned, staring vacantly at it; it was not much to see but, really, it was all that anyone had seen or was likely to see of the Martians. All these reporters and cameramen and columnists and sound men, thought Mr Mandala with pleasure, all of them waiting here for the ten AM briefing at the Cape would have a forty-mile drive through the palmetto swamps for nothing. Because what they would see when they got there would be just about what they were seeing now.

One of the poker players was telling a long, involved joke about Martians wearing fur coats at Miami Beach. Mr Mandala looked at them with dislike. If only some of them would go to their rooms and go to sleep he might try asking the others if they were registered in the motel. Although actually he couldn't squeeze anyone else in anyway, with all the rooms doubly occupied already. He gave up the thought and stared vacantly at the Martians on the screen, trying to imagine people all over the world looking at that picture on their television sets, reading about them in their newspapers, *caring* about them. They did not look worth caring about as they sluggishly crawled about on their long, weak limbs, like a stretched seal's flippers, gasping heavily in the drag of Earth's gravity, their great long eyes dull.

'Stupid-looking little bastards,' one of the reporters said to the pipe-smoker. 'You know what I heard? I heard the reason the astronauts kept them locked in the back was the stink.'

'They probably don't notice it on Mars,' said the pipe-smoker judiciously. 'Thin air.'

'Notice it? They love it.' He dropped a dollar bill on the desk in front of Mr Mandala. 'Can I have change for the Coke machine?' Mr Mandala counted out dimes silently. It had not occurred to him that the Martians would smell, but that was only because he hadn't given it much of a thought. If he had thought about it at all, that was what he would have thought.

Mr Mandala fished out a dime for himself and followed the two men over to the Coke machine. The picture on the TV changed to some rather poorly photographed shots brought back by the astronauts, of low, irregular sand-coloured buildings on a bright sand floor. These were what NASA was calling 'the largest Martian city', altogether about a hundred of the flat, windowless structures. 'I dunno,' said the second reporter at last, tilting his Coke bottle. 'You think they're what you'd call intelligent?'

'Difficult to say, exactly,' said the pipe-smoker. He was from Reuter's and looked it, with a red, broad English squire's face. 'They do build houses,' he pointed out.

'So does a bull gorilla.'

'No doubt. No doubt.' The Reuter's man brightened. 'Oh just a moment. That makes me think of one. There once was – let me see, at home we tell it about the Irish – yes, I have it. The next spaceship goes to Mars, you see, and they find that some dread terrestrial disease has wiped out the whole race, all but one female. These fellows too, gone. All gone except this one she. Well, they're terribly upset, and they debate it at the UN and start an anti-genocide pact and America votes two hundred million dollars for reparations and, well, the long and short of it is, in order to keep the race from dying out entirely they decide to breed a non-human man to this one surviving Martian female.'

'Cripes!'

'Yes, exactly. Well, then they find Paddy O'Shaughnessy, down on his luck and they say to him, "See here, just go in that cage there, Paddy, and you'll find this female. And all you've got to do is render her pregnant, do you see?" And O'Shaughnessy says, "What's in it for me?" and they offer him, oh, thousands of pounds. And of course he agrees. But then he opens the door of the cage and he sees what the female looks like. And he backs out.' The Reuter's man replaced his empty Coke bottle in the rack and grimaced, showing Paddy's expression of revulsion. '"Holy saints," he says, "I never counted on anything like this." "Thousands of pounds, Paddy!" they say to him, urging him on. "Oh, very well, then," he says, "but on one condition." "And what may that be?" they ask him. "You've got to promise me," he says, "that the children'll be raised in the Church."'

'Yeah, I heard that,' said the other reporter. And he moved to put his bottle back, and as he did his foot caught in the rack and four cases of empty Coke bottles bounced and clattered across the floor.

Well, that was just about more than Mr Mandala could stand and he gasped, stuttered, dinged his bell and shouted, 'Ernest! Berzie! On the double!' And when Ernest showed up, poking his dark plum-coloured head out of the service door with an expression that revealed an anticipation of disaster, Mr Mandala shouted: 'Oh, curse your thick heads, I told you a hundred times, keep those racks cleaned out.' And he stood over the two bellmen, fuming, as they bent to the litter of whole bottles and broken glass, their faces glancing up at him sidewise, worried, dark plum and Arabian sand. He knew that all the reporters were looking at him and that they disapproved.

And then he went out into the late night to cool off, because he was sorry and knew he might make himself still sorrier.

The grass was wet. Condensing dew was dripping from the fittings of the diving board into the pool. The motel was not as quiet as it should be so close to dawn, but it was quiet enough. There was only an occasional distant laugh, and the noise from the lounge. To Mr Mandala it was reassuring. He replenished his soul by walking all the galleries around the rooms, checking the ice makers and the cigarette machines, and finding that all was well.

A military jet from McCoy was screaming overhead. Beyond it the stars were still bright, in spite of the beginnings of dawn in the east. Mr Mandala yawned, glanced mildly up and wondered which of them was Mars, and returned to his desk; and shortly he was too busy with the long, exhausting round of room calls and check-outs to think about Martians. Then, when most of the guests were getting noisily into their cars and limobuses and the day men were coming on, Mr Mandala uncapped two cold Cokes and carried one back through the service door to Ernest.

'Rough night,' he said, and Ernest, accepting both the Coke and the intention, nodded and drank it down. They leaned against the wall that screened the pool from the access road and watched the newsmen and newsgirls taking off down the road towards the highway and the ten o'clock briefing. Most of them had had no sleep. Mr Mandala shook his head, disapproving so much commotion for so little cause.

And Ernest snapped his fingers, grinned and said, 'I got a Martian joke, Mr Mandala. What do you call a seven-foot Martian when he's comin' at you with a spear?'

'Oh, hell, Ernest,' said Mr Mandala, 'you call him sir. Everybody knows that one.' He yawned and stretched and said reflectively, 'You'd think there'd be some new jokes. All I heard was the old ones, only instead of picking on the Jews and the Catholics and – and everybody, they were telling them about the Martians.'

'Yeah, I noticed that, Mr Mandala,' said Ernest.

Mr Mandala stood up. 'Better get some sleep,' he advised, 'because they might all be back again tonight. I don't know what for... Know what I think, Ernest? Outside of the jokes, I don't think that six months from now anybody's going to remember there ever were such things as Martians. I don't believe their coming here is going to make a nickel's worth of difference to anybody.'

'Hate to disagree with you, Mr Mandala,' said Ernest mildly, 'but I don't think so. Going to make a difference to some people. Going to make a *damn* big difference to me.'

SCHEMATIC MAN

I KNOW I'M not really a funny man, but I don't like other people to know it. I do what other people without much sense of humour do: I tell jokes. If we're sitting next to each other at a faculty senate and I want to introduce myself, I probably say: 'Bederkind is my name, and computers are my game.'

Nobody laughs much. Like all my jokes, it needs to be explained. The joking part is that it was through game theory that I first became interested in computers and the making of mathematical models. Sometimes when I'm explaining it, I say there that the mathematical ones are the only models I've ever had a chance to make. That gets a smile, anyway. I've figured out why: even if you don't really get much out of the play on words, you can tell it's got something to do with sex, and we all reflexively smile when anybody says anything sexy.

I ought to tell you what a mathematical model is, right? All right. It's simple. It's a kind of picture of something made out of numbers. You use it because it's easier to make numbers move than to make real things move.

Suppose I want to know what the planet Mars is going to do over the next few years. I take everything I know about Mars and I turn it into numbers – a number for its speed in orbit, another number for how much it weighs, another number for how many miles it is in diameter, another number to express how strongly the Sun pulls it towards it and all that. Then I tell the computer that's all it needs to know about Mars, and I go on to tell it all the same sorts of numbers about the Earth, about Venus, Jupiter, the Sun itself – about all the other chunks of matter floating around in the neighbourhood that I think are likely to make any difference to Mars. I then teach the computer some simple rules about how the set of numbers that represent Jupiter say, affect the numbers that represent Mars: the law of inverse squares, some rules of celestial mechanics, a few relativistic corrections – well, actually, there are a lot of things it needs to know. But not more than I can tell it.

When I have done all this – not exactly in English but in a kind of language that it knows how to handle – the computer has a mathematical model of Mars stored inside it. It will then whirl its mathematical Mars through mathematical space for as many orbits as I like. I say to it, '1997 June 18th 24.00 GMT,' and it . . . it . . . well, I guess the word for it is, it *imagines* where Mars will be, relative to my back-yard Questar, at midnight Greenwich time on June 18th, 1997, and tells me which way to point.

It isn't real Mars that it plays with. It's a mathematical model, you see. But for the purposes of knowing where to point my little telescope, it does everything that 'real Mars' would do for me, only much faster. I don't have to wait for 1997; I can find out in five minutes.

It isn't only planets that can carry on a mathematical metalife in the memory banks of a computer. Take my friend Schmuel. He has a joke, too, and his joke is that he makes twenty babies a day in his computer. What he means by that is that, after six years of trying, he finally succeeded in writing down the numbers that describe the development of a human baby in its mother's uterus, all the way from conception to birth. The point of that is that then it was comparatively easy to write down the numbers for a lot of things that happen to babies before they're born. Momma has high blood pressure. Momma smokes three packs a day. Momma catches scarlet fever or a kick in the belly. Momma keeps making it with Poppa every night until they wheel her into the delivery room. And so on. And the point of *that* is that this way, Schmuel can see some of the things that go wrong and make some babies get born retarded, or blind or with retrolentol fibroplasia or an inability to drink cow's milk. It's easier than sacrificing a lot of pregnant women and cutting them open to see.

OK, you don't want to hear any more about mathematical models, because what kicks are there in mathematical models for you? I'm glad you asked. Consider a for instance. For instance, suppose last night you were watching the *Late, Late* and you saw Carole Lombard, or maybe Marilyn Monroe with that dinky little skirt blowing up over those pretty thighs. I assume you know that these ladies are dead. I also assume that your glands responded to those cathode-tube flickers as though they were alive. And so you do get some kicks from mathematical models, because each of those great girls, in each of their poses and smiles, was nothing but a number of some thousands of digits, expressed as a spot of light on a phosphor tube. With some added numbers to express the frequency patterns of their voices. Nothing else.

And the point of *that* (how often I use that phrase!) is that a mathematical model not only represents the real thing but sometimes it's as good as the real thing. No, honestly. I mean, do you really believe that if it had been Marilyn or Carole in the flesh you were looking at, across a row of floodlights, say, that you could have taken away any more of them than you gleaned from the shower of electrons that made the phosphors display their pictures?

I did watch Marilyn on the *Late, Late* one night. And I thought those thoughts; and so I spent the next week preparing an application to a foundation for money; and when the grant came through, I took a sabbatical and began turning myself into a mathematical model. It isn't really that hard. Kookie, yes. But not hard.

I don't want to explain what programmes like FORTRAN and SIMSCRIPT and SIR are, so I will only say what we all say: they are languages by which people can communicate with machines. Sort of. I had to learn to speak FORTRAN well enough to tell the machine all about myself. It took five graduate students and ten months to write the programme that made that possible, but that's not much. It took more than that to teach a computer to shoot pool. After that, it was just a matter of storing myself in the machine.

That's the part that Schmuel told me was kookie. Like everybody with enough seniority in my department, I have a remote-access computer console in my – well, I called it my 'playroom'. I did have a party there, once, right after I bought the house, when I still thought I was going to get married. Schmuel caught me one night walking in the door and down the stairs and finding me methodically typing out my medical history from the ages of four to fourteen. 'Jerk,' he said, 'what makes you think you deserve to be embalmed in a 7094?'

I said, 'Make some coffee and leave me alone till I finish. Listen. Can I use your programme on the sequelae of mumps?'

'Paranoid psychosis,' he said. 'It comes on about the age of forty-two.' But he coded the console for me and thus gave me access to his programmes. I finished and said:

'Thanks for the programme, but you make rotten coffee.'

'You make rotten jokes. You really think it's going to be *you* in that programme. Admit!'

By then, I had most of the basic physiological and environmental stuff on the tapes and I was feeling good. 'What's me?' I asked. 'If it talks like me, and thinks like me, and remembers what I remember, and does what I would do – who is it? President Eisenhower?'

'Eisenhower was years ago, jerk,' he said.

'Turing's question, Schmuel,' I said. 'If I'm in one room with a teletype. And the computer's in another room with a teletype, programmed to model me. And you're in a third room, connected to both teletypes, and you have a conversation with both of us, and you can't tell which is me and which is the machine – then how do you describe the difference? *Is* there a difference?'

He said, 'The difference, Josiah, is I can touch you. And smell you. If I was crazy enough I could kiss you. You. Not the model.'

'You could,' I said, 'if you were a model, too, and were in the machine with me.' And I joked with him (Look! It solves the population problem, put everybody in the machine. And, suppose I get cancer. Flesh-me dies. Mathematical-model-me just rewrites its programme), but he was really worried. He really did think I was going crazy, but I perceived that his reasons were not because of the nature of the problem but because of what he fancied was my own attitude towards it, and I made up my mind to be careful of what I said to Schmuel.

So I went on playing Turing's game, trying to make the computer's responses indistinguishable from my own. I instructed it in what a toothache felt like and what I remembered of sex. I taught it memory links betweeen people and phone numbers, and all the state capitals I had won a prize for knowing when I was ten. I trained it to spell 'rhythm' wrong, as I had always misspelled it, and to say 'place' instead of 'put' in conversation, as I have always done because of the slight speech impediment that carried over from my adolescence. I played that game; and by God, I won it.

But I don't know for sure what I lost in exchange.

I know I lost something.

I began by losing parts of my memory. When my cousin Alvin from Cleveland phoned me on my birthday, I couldn't remember who he was for a minute. (The week before, I had told the computer all about my summers with Alvin's family, including the afternoon when we both lost our virginity to the same girl, under the bridge by my uncle's farm.) I had to write down Schmuel's phone number, and my secretary's, and carry them around in my pocket.

As the work progressed, I lost more. I looked up at the sky one night and saw three bright stars in a line overhead. It scared me, because I didn't know what they were until I got home and took out my sky charts. Yet Orion was my first and easiest constellation. And when I looked at the telescope I had made, I could not remember how I had figured the mirror.

Schmuel kept warning me about overwork. I really was working a lot, fifteen hours a day and more. But it didn't feel like overwork. It felt as though I were losing pieces of myself. I was not merely teaching the computer to be me but putting pieces of me into the computer. I hated that, and it shook me enough to make me take the whole of Christmas week off. I went to Miami.

But when I got back to work, I couldn't remember how to touch-type on the console any more and was reduced to pecking out information for the computer a letter at a time. I felt as though I were moving from one place to another in instalments, and not enough of me had arrived yet to be a quorum, but what was still waiting to go had important parts missing. And yet I continued to pour myself into the magnetic memory cores: the lie I told my draft board in 1946, the limerick I made up about my first wife after the divorce, what Margaret wrote when she told me she wouldn't marry me.

There was plenty of room in the storage banks for all of it. The computer could hold all my brain had held, especially with the programme my five graduate students and I had written. I had been worried about that, at first.

But in the event I did not run out of room. What I ran out of was myself. I remember feeling sort of opaque and stunned and empty; and that is all I remember until now.

Whenever 'now' is.

I had another friend once, and he cracked up while working on telemetry studies for one of the Mariner programmes. I remember going to see him in the hospital, and him telling me, in his slow, unworried, coked-up voice, what they had done for him. Or to him. Electroshock. Hydrotherapy.

What worries me is that that is at least a reasonable working hypothesis to describe what is happening to me now.

I remember, or think I remember, a sharp electric jolt. I

feel, or think I feel, a chilling flow around me.

What does it mean? I wish I were sure. I'm willing to concede that it might mean that overwork did me in and now I, too, am at Restful Retreat, being studied by the psychiatrists and changed by the nurses' aides. Willing to concede it? Dear God, I *pray* for it. I pray that that electricity was just shock therapy and not something else. I pray that the flow I feel is water sluicing around my sodden sheets and not a flux of electrons in transistor modules. I don't fear the thought of being insane; I fear the alternative.

I do not *believe* the alternative. But I fear it all the same. I can't believe that all that's left of me – my id, my ucs, my *me* – is nothing but a mathematical model stored inside the banks of the 7094. But if I am! If I am, dear God, what will happen when – and how can I wait until – somebody turns me on?

SMALL LORDS

I

CLITEMAN PICKED HIS way mincingly along the greenish sands of the beach. It was nearly dark. and that made it bad, because he had to watch where he was stepping. The crazy young ones were just as likely as not to run across his path for a thrill. And if he missed seeing one in the dusk, and stepped on it.

He swallowed and moved closer to the water's edge. It might be best, everything considered, to swim back; but he didn't like the thought of that brackish water in the sores on his back. The foreman had given him an unusually hard time that day – well, maybe the foreman's wife had given *him* a hard time that morning and he was just taking it out on Cliteman. If the foreman had a wife.

Cliteman stopped at the outskirts of the little village he called Salt Lake City and whistled, as he had learned it was best to do. The greenish, jewel-like lights in the windows of the tiny houses were all on; and the larger, bluer lights in the streets gave Cliteman a pretty good view, even though the light from setting Canopus was rapidly dwindling.

Cliteman saw that one of the midges was waving at him, and he squatted down. The midge was big for its race, very nearly half an inch tall. It stood on two legs like a man; it had two arms like a man, and a head like a man's head. The glossy eyes that covered nearly the whole head were not a man's, of course, and the shrill, piping voice was closer to the stridulations of an insect.

It was waving him away from the village off the beach. Cliteman saw why; there was some sort of gathering on the sands, several hundreds of the midges. Without resentment, he waded into the shallows and around the town, though the sting of the water on his scarred legs was extremely painful.

But that wasn't important to Cliteman at the moment. What was important was that he was almost unbearably hungry. If only Morris had found something decent to eat for a change! A couple of dozen of the big pink shellfish perhaps, or one of those big, six-legged swimming things that tasted faintly of peach-pits...

Splat. Cliteman yelled involuntarily as the biting greenish spark charred a tiny crater in his shoulder. One of the midges was standing threateningly on a rock in his path aiming at him with the glistening small hand weapons that they used for disciplining the Earthmen – or for killing each other as the occasion arose.

Splat. Another spark flared close by, this one only a warning. Cliteman clutched his shoulder and, ever so gently, moved farther out into the water. It was important not to move quickly; the spray a fast-moving foot might kick up was enough to drown a midge.

And that was about all he needed. If he killed one of them, that would be the end of everything. Cliteman vividly remembered what had happened to Fuller when he had crushed one of the little aliens. Quite by accident; but the aliens either didn't know that, or didn't care.

It wasn't that they were deliberately cruel in the way they destroyed Fuller; or at least, Cliteman thought it wasn't. But these beings were tiny and humans huge; they had only tiny weapons against the gross flesh monoliths from the exploring ship. Death at the hands of the midges was like death from an army of raging termites. It came with a hundred, a thousand, ten thousand little, painful, finally fatal wounds. Perhaps there weren't any good ways to die, Cliteman thought, but certainly there were few that were worse.

As quickly as he could, Cliteman hurried down the brackish sea's shore, each step a carefully planned, meticulously executed problem in engineering. He tried to stay ankle-deep in the water, away from possible wandering midges on the beach, but not so deep that his steps would splash any who might come by. The foot carefully lifted and carefully brought forward; the toe pointed out just so, slipped into the water ahead as delicately as the top liqueur in a *pousse-café*.

Just ahead was the little cape the aliens had indicated the human giants might use for their own, free and clear. 'Morris!' cried Cliteman. 'Hello there!'

No answer; not even the gleam of firelight, where Morris should already have had the fire going, cooking whatever he had been able to turn up in the way of food. Morris was the official provider for the humans, permitted by the tiny aliens to labour only half a day on the crude projects they had assigned the others, so that he might have time to find and prepare the enormous masses of food the giants required. 'Morris! Are you there?'

But he wasn't there. Cliteman was alone.

Canopus was down now, and the only light was from the bluish star they called Neighbour. From Earth, Neighbour was only a tiny spot of light – twelfth magnitude or thereabouts – smaller than the 200-inch telescope. But it happened to hang close in space to the system of Canopus. Though its absolute magnitude was only four or five times the brightness of the sun, it was close enough so that in the night sky it seemed brighter than Earth's moon, bright enough to see by, uncomfortably bright to look at direct.

There was not, however, light enough to make it easy for Cliteman to tend his nets. After half an hour he hauled in his catch; something throbbed and leaped in the purse. He pulled on the long, precious ropes with his mouth watering, it wasn't until he had the net on the sand, maddeningly empty, that he saw he had neglected to fasten the other end. The prey had escaped; he grimly tied the necessary knots, and cast it out again.

Cliteman lay down on the beach to wait. It was getting chilly – the planet's air was thin. Canopus provided plenty of heat by day, but with the setting of their sun the temperature dropped thirty or forty degrees in as many minutes. The fire was a comfort, but of course it didn't do to make it large – everything on the planet's surface was on a smallish scale; the largest vegetation not much taller than a man. Already in only a few months, they had nearly denuded the little cape that was set aside for them of burnable brush, and there was no way of knowing if the midges would permit them to extend their foraging inland. The trouble was, they couldn't talk to the midges. It was not merely a matter of language, but the auditory range of the little aliens was pitched bat-high; only the sharpest whistles of the Earthmen could be heard by the midges – as bass rumbles, no doubt.

Cliteman stared wearily at Neighbour through half-closed eyes. Somewhere about Neighbour, the interstellar ship would be orbiting now, while its scout rockets surveyed the half-dozen planets they had located from space. The ship had been gone six months; it would be gone six months more, at least.

There was a grave doubt in Cliteman's mind that any of them would survive another six months of this.

There had been ten men in the scout rocket that set down on Canopus' sixth planet. Three were dead – Fuller under the weapons of the midges, Breck and Hogarth when the rocket crashed. Morris was sick – it was no charity that made the midges let him have his half-day off; even the tiny aliens could see that the radioman was in bad shape.

And the rest of them were slaves.

Something whistled through the air high overhead – a hundred yards or more. Cliteman instinctively stood up and raised his hand to identify himself. It was a midge flyer, one of the foot-long jets that he had seen from time to time on mysterious errands, no doubt diverted from whatever course it had been pursuing by the sight of his fire. It circled with a thin noise like a swinging whip, and Cliteman saw the pattern of coloured lights on its dragonfly wings that seemed to be an identification marking. 'Take a good look!' he mumbled to himself. He looked more closely himself, and saw that this particular jet was much smaller than others he had seen. It couldn't have been more than three or four inches long, he guessed, as it spiralled down within a few yards of his head. No doubt a one-'man' ship, to be used for – for...

Cliteman lowered his hands sourly, craning his neck to stare down the shore where Morris should have been coming, but wasn't. He didn't *know* what the midges might use a one-man jet for. Did they have wars? Perhaps; and perhaps a small jet might be a fighter. But it was only a guess, and the chances were extremely good that any guess any of the Earthmen might make about the midges was quite wrong. There had been no chance to learn; the scout rocket had come in without orbiting – though no amount of orbiting would have done much good, since no conceivable midge installation would have been visible from space. They had observed nothing in the descent, beyond the bare outlines of the planet's geography; they had crashed in landing, and had stumbled out into an aroused hornet's nest of mighty little warriors.

And from then on, nothing.

The tiny jet whipped once more around him and shot out over the water. Cliteman touched his sore shoulder with a gentle hand, staring absently after it.

Then he focused his eyes and his attention. Something was floundering in the net.

Dinner! He jumped for the ropes that he and Morris had so painstakingly pieced together and pulled the purse towards the shore. Whatever it was that was in the net, it was of a size that promised a full meal! Be damned to Morris, Cliteman thought rebelliously; let him go hungry then! He carefully jockeyed the net into the shallows, and in Neighbour's blue-white light he saw the thrashing sea-creature's struggles break the surface of the water. He played it as any angler plays a trout, fully concentrated, aware of nothing but his net and his prey...

Disastrously aware of nothing; for disaster came.

He heard, a little too late, the deeper, slower whistle of the jet again. He looked up a little too late, and saw it settling down towards the water, close inshore, just beyond his net.

The jet's tiny pilot was landing!

Cliteman pulled frantically at the ropes; then dropped them. Too late! The jet seemed to falter and swerve, as though the pilot had at last seen the treacherous snarl of ropes, and the leaping sea-creature in the water before him. Too late. The tiny aircraft had already touched its narrow keel to the water; it bounced on one cord and spun around another; it ploughed into the tangle of the net itself and flipped over.

Cliteman, panicky, leapt knee-deep into the water and clutched at the doll-sized aircraft. He roared and jerked his hands away; stupid of him to have touched the jet exhaust! He grasped it gently around the middle of the fuselage and lifted it, held it in his hand, staring. It was impossible to see the pilot in only the light from Neighbour; in a moment he brought it to the fire and set it down on a little rock, and knelt to peer inside the little transparent hatch.

The pilot was inside, all right; but motionless. Unconscious, perhaps, or dead.

In either case, there was no doubt in Cliteman's mind that he was in trouble.

2

Morris limped slowly towards the reservation.

He was hungry, in spite of the wearing, burning pain in his chest that had been getting worse ever since the rocket crash; and he was bone-tired. His whole back was a pattern of new scars as well; it had taken quite a few applications of the midges' weapons before he understood that this day was not like all the other days, that this day the midges did not intend to permit him to leave his work halfway through the day. The scars were the penalty he had to pay for not understanding; but it didn't make them less painful.

Besides, there would be trouble with Cliteman, Morris knew with resignation. How close to the beast they had all returned! Take the case of Sanford Cliteman, lieutenant in the Space Force, respected citizen, loved husband and father of two. Morris had played many a game of chess with Cliteman on the way out, the lieutenant had been a skilled opponent, generous in victory, good-natured in defeat.

Yet, what about the time three days before when Morris had torn the net and there had been no dinner ready for Cliteman? The man's anger had been animal – and Morris himself had flared into anger in response; the two of them had come close to a fist-fight. Animal!

But how could they help it? They were treated as beasts, mindless prime movers suitable for clearing land for the strange midge farms, or for scrabbling at the earth to make culverts and irrigation ditches. If they offended, they were given a beast's punishment, a touch of the whip. If they served well, they got a beast's reward, to be turned loose at sundown – free to feed and sleep. That was the greatest gift the midges ever gave.

'Why?' Morris demanded, puffing and holding his bad leg as he limped along. It seemed impossible that the midges should not realize they were intelligent, highly civilized beings. They had seen the rocket; they could not imagine beasts could create or man such a machine. But there was simply no sign of an attempt at communication.

In the fury of the first fight, the Earthmen had been completely off guard. The rocket had crashed; that put an end to the book's rules about the first contact on an alien planet. They had stumbled out of the wreck, mostly unharmed, mostly hurt or shaken up. They had been greeted with fire from the midge hand weapons, and even more serious fire from what might have been the equivalent of self-propelled artillery. Well, maybe they should have reacted quicker, Morris thought; they could have stuck together, leaped back into the rocket in spite of the threat of fire and explosion, armed themselves, fought off the aliens. But in the split second when that was still possible they had wavered.

Carrasquel had drawn his gun and begun return fire; but the equation one bullet – one midge did not balance to the advantage of the Earthmen. Undoubtedly Carrasquel had killed a few, but what was the use of killing a few – or a hundred – or a thousand? Fuller hadn't a gun, but he had stamped at them as though they were insects. It was Fuller the midges destroyed, in cold blood, while he lay in helpless anguish under the shock of their concentrated fire. Concentrated, that was it; the midges had leaped into action, each group fixed firmly on a target; the humans in their surprise had blundered and scattered. And they never had really got together again. The midge tactics had evidently been to keep them apart, for the fire was most punishing when any two of the Earthmen tried to come together...

And now there was Cliteman and himself, who had been driven miles and miles across country, under the stings of the pursuing midges in their vehicles and their aircraft. He knew where Carrasquel and Boehm were, because he'd chanced to see Boehm and they'd been able to shout to each other for a moment; the others he hadn't even seen in months.

But if only the midges had waited – if only the midges had tried to make contact, come to appreciate that Earthmen were their superiors, in any imaginable scale of intellectual values...

But come to think of it, Morris told himself dourly, that was no longer so very true.

Morris laboured around the little hill that went down to the water and saw Cliteman fiddling with something on the ground. There was no smell of cooking fish; there was something wrong. 'Cliteman, what's the matter?'

The lieutenant jumped up, startled, his eyes wild. Then he saw who it was. 'Oh, Morris. This damn midge – Where the hell have you been? I've been starving – Never mind that. Look what I've got here!'

Morris looked, and opened his eyes, and looked again. He whispered, 'Sweet love of heaven!'

'What am I going to do?' Cliteman demanded. 'Look at the damn things, Morris. They're hurt! They might be dying, for all I know.'

'They?'

Cliteman said bitterly, 'Three of them; three little midges, out for a little excursion. Momma Midge and Poppa Midge and Little Bitty Baby Midge – I guess. And what do you think they'll make of that, Morris? I've been sitting here trying to make up my mind to chuck them back in the drink.'

'No, Cliteman!'

Cliteman stared at him woodenly for a second. 'Remember Fuller?' he asked for a moment.

'I know, Cliteman, but...'

'They'll think *I* killed them! And how do I know? Maybe I did. If I hadn't been pulling in the net just when they landed their stinking plane it would have been all right! But here they are, and do you know what comes next, Morris? Because I don't!'

Morris lowered himself gingerly to the ground – something he was reluctant to do, because it wasn't always easy getting up again. 'Shut up a minute,' he ordered, and looked closely at the midge plane.

There were three of them in it, all right. Two stirring faintly, one motionless. Dead? Morris had no idea. They all had their eyes open, but as far as Morris or Cliteman knew, midges had nothing to close their eyes with; neither of them had ever seen one blink. The transparent canopy was smashed open. Apparently, Cliteman's first frantic idea was to get the three of them out of the plane, but once he'd opened the canopy he hadn't dared touch them.

Morris stared dazedly at the tiny machine. It was a beautifully made child's toy; any kid on Earth would have given his chance of immortality for one like it. Three inches long, five inches from wingtip to where the other wingtip would have been if it hadn't been crumpled flat. It was still in working condition except for the wings and the canopy – at any rate, tiny red and purple lights winked on what might have been the instrument panel, and something that Morris couldn't see was making a faint, high-pitched hum.

Morris propped himself on an elbow and ventured to touch one of the midges with a delicately questing finger. It moved slightly, but whether it was cold to the touch, or warm he couldn't have said.

He noticed silvery threads and rods, so small they were almost invisible, tangled in a little heap on a flat rock beside the ship. 'What's that?'

Cliteman took a deep breath. He sounded a little more human as he said, 'I don't know. I thought they might be – well, radio antennae or something. I broke them off. Didn't want them calling for help.'

Morris shook his head. Cliteman cried, 'Don't tell me I shouldn't have done that! Maybe I shouldn't have, but – curse it, Morris, I was scared! Don't forget Fuller.'

Morris sighed. He said wearily, 'I'm hungry,' and pushed himself to a sitting position, still looking at the little plane. 'They kept me working till dark,' he said absently. 'I guess they decided I'm well enough to put in a full day's work now. Or maybe that I'm not well enough to be worth pampering – might as well work me to death. I don't suppose you caught anything to eat?'

'Morris, don't you see what trouble we're in?'

Morris looked at Cliteman soberly. 'They'll blame us for sure!' Morris noted that it was 'us' who had become responsible for what had happened to the midge plane. 'Look, Morris, the way I see it there are only two things we can do. One, we can get rid of it – sink it in the ocean, and hope they never find it. Maybe they won't. Maybe they won't connect us with what happened to the plane.'

'And maybe they will,' said Morris.

'All right, they will,' Cliteman agreed. 'Sure, why kid ourselves? So that only leaves one thing. It's time for us to make our break, Morris. Like we talked about. We'll cut straight across the country till we find that big river and stay right with it. It can't be more than ten miles. We won't miss the rocket, it's too big. What do you say, Morris? We've been planning to do it anyhow as soon as you were feeling better. Well, this just moves the date up. We can't wait. It's too big a risk, Morris; remember Fuller. What about it? If we...'

'Shut up.' Cliteman blinked and stared. 'No, *shut up*!' Morris sat straight, peering at the sky. It wasn't anger that had made him tell the lieutenant to shut up, although he felt something that came close to anger.

He had heard something.

He listened; the two of them listened.

They heard it, and then in a moment they saw: the faint whistle, the patterned lights of a midge jet circling overhead.

3

'Act busy!' cried Cliteman. 'Start putting wood on the fire!'

He himself leaped towards the net, where the neglected fish-thing was feebly flapping away what remained of its strength. He drew it in while Morris laboriously got to his feet and fed the fire. Cliteman grasped the slippery creature, reckless of possible teeth or stinging spines. He bashed it expertly against a rock and then took a closer look at it. It was tentacled, not much over a foot long and plump as a frog's belly. Cliteman quickly skewered it on a gnarled stem of green wood and handed it to Morris to broil.

'But you didn't clean it!' Morris protested. 'We can't eat this without...'

'Cook it! We aren't going to eat it, you idiot. Just look busy until that damn plane goes away.'

Cliteman glanced warily up. It was still there, perhaps not as close, but well within the range of the sound its jets made. He swore under his breath, looked around undecidedly, and settled on adding more fuel to the fire. He bent down for branches, and abruptly jumped up as though he had seen an adder. 'What's the matter?' Morris demanded, startled.

'That thing!' Cliteman's voice was shaky. He was staring at the wrecked midge flyer on the ground before him. He darted a quick look over his shoulder, then jumped towards it, obviously intending to stamp it into the ground.

'Wait!' screamed Morris; blocking Cliteman's path.

'Out of the way!'

'No, Cliteman! You'll kill them!'

'You're damn well right I'll kill them. We're crazy to leave that thing in plain sight. Those others will come back any minute, and if they see it, wham! We're done for, man!'

'Wait!' ordered Morris in a totally different voice, a voice of command.

Cliteman stopped and stared.

Morris said tightly, 'It's murder. I won't let you do it.'

Cliteman stood poised, and his eyes were hard on the limping man. He held the twisted stick of firewood in his hand. For a moment it seemed that the stick would be a club, to strike at Morris; but there was a nearing whistle and a fleck of light that darted about their heads. Both men jumped. They had forgotten the midge jet, but the jet had not forgotten them. It came swooping in on them like an Earthly plane circling living pylons; and if there had been a chance before, that chance was gone.

Perhaps it had been only curiosity that made the midge pilot come close to the quarrelling Titans; perhaps he had caught a glimpse of the wreck. Whatever, it did him in; for the stick that might have been a club became a flyswatter; Cliteman swung, as quickly, as thoughtlessly as a polar relay, and slapped the prying midge plane out of the air. There was a faint ringing crunch as the tree trunk hit the plane, and a distant hiss and tiny crack as the plane slammed into the water and exploded; and that was the end of that.

'Now we are in for it,' said Cliteman after a moment. And, after a moment more, 'I'm sorry.'

Morris only shook his head. It was late to be sorry. 'Clean that fish, will you?' he said.

'Clean— What?'

'That fish,' said Morris irritably. 'Or whatever it is. We're going to have to eat it, you know. We're going to have a long night ahead of us.'

He turned his back on the other man and bent to look at the crashed midge flyer that had started the trouble. They were alive after all, he saw absently; all three of the occupants were moving and one of them was chirping excitedly. Not that it mattered to Morris, not any more ...

Picture a pair of horrid monsters, obelisk-tall, deformed beyond human experience, rampaging about Levittown or thundering in the surf at Laguna Beach. Picture them dropped from space in a queer, enormous vessel the like of which no man had ever seen, their voices a quivering diapason that hurts the ear and shakes the spine. Picture them feasting on whale sharks or such enormous offal from the sea, quarrelling among themselves, and striking out to clout an airliner in ruins from the sky.

It is no wonder, though Morris, *that the midges don't want us around.*

But if the positions had been reversed – would we at least have tried to communicate?

But – if the positions had been reversed – would we have allowed the monsters to live at all?

Morris sighed, and blew on the chunk of greasy flesh he was holding, and forced himself to eat.

The two men ate in silence. Above them, and outward to the sea, there was a clustering swarm of midge aircraft, not approaching, but observing every move. They had begun to arrive within minutes after Cliteman had struck at the midge plane. They were waiting for something.

Whatever it was it couldn't be long in coming.

'Hurry up!' Cliteman grumbled hoarsely. Morris nodded but didn't answer; there wasn't much to say.

They had planned for a month, and the sum of their planning was this: some day they would make a break for the rocket. It would not be impossible, for between them and the spot where the rocket had crashed lay dense brush – towering jungle, by midge standards; it would be hard for the little creatures to bring much force to bear against them. On the other hand, it would not be very fruitful, for the rocket had crashed. As a plan, it had only one real advantage; it was better than nothing.

It would have been better, thought Morris with detachment, *if we could have waited until I was stronger – until the ship returned from Neighbour, and maybe another rocket might come down – until the chances were somehow better . . .*

But that was exactly what was no longer possible. For there was no doubt that whatever the Earthmen's status with the midges had been, the destruction of the plane had changed it for the worse.

'Morris! What the devil's that?'

Cliteman was pointing.

Something bright and fast was gliding towards them in the water. It was long – six or eight feet, easily – but not very wide. It looked rather like a mechanized small canoe, with a row of lights and brighter lights fixed forward.

Hiss, *splat.* A fat blue spark leaped from the prow of the thing towards them, fell short and sizzled in the water.

'I didn't know the midges had battleships,' said Morris in amazement, and then shook himself. 'Come on; let's get out of here!'

'Hold it!' Cliteman caught him by the shoulder, his eyes huge and fearful as he stared down the beach. In the pale light from Neighbour it was hard to see what was going on. But once again there were lights, hundreds of them it seemed; they dipped and bobbed and joggled and came on. Morris saw at last what the lights belonged to. They were wheeled machines – not Earthly wheels, thin in proportion to their diameter, but constructed like flabby steam-rollers, creeping forward on rubbery cylinders. There were scores and hundreds of them. Tanks? Something like tanks, at any rate; in a moment they opened fire, too, and the giants from Earth were caught in a criss-cross of flying sparks. '*We're cut off!*' cried Cliteman. '*Run!*'

But it was a little late to run.

A fat blue spark caught Cliteman on the shoulder and spun him around, yelling. Morris dropped to the ground as another hissed past him, and he could smell the dry, chemical bite of ozone in his nose, taste the metallic eddy-currents in his teeth. 'They can see us in the firelight!' Cliteman yelled, and began to kick furiously at the little campfire. Burning sticks scattered into the brush, sparks flew up from the fire – redder, milder sparks than those that came from the midge weapons, but sparks that could burn all the same.

The fire from the midge tanks on the beach came in thick volleys now, and it was impossible that all of them should miss. These were no mere bee-stings like the hand weapons, Morris discovered; he yelled, holding his arm, as he discovered it. A couple of shots from these heavy weapons could easily kill.

He lifted his head. 'We've got to get out of here! Look!' The flying brands from the fire had not conveniently gone out; the brush was beginning to blaze.

'It'll give them something to think about,' Cliteman snarled, and plunged towards the mainland, bobbing and weaving and yelling. It was miraculous that he wasn't struck down by the massed fire from the beach – yet perhaps not so miraculous, for what human gunners could have kept their heads in the face of a charging, bellowing monster a tenth of a mile tall? He got free, Morris following, and in a moment they were in the momentary shelter of the deep brush inland. Behind them, yellow flames and floating sparks rose up towards the bright night sky; ahead was only darkness.

Morris leaned against a twelve-foot tree, panting hoarsely. 'What – what next?' he gasped, fighting for breath.

Cliteman breathed a long, shuddering sigh. 'What do you think? We'll try for the rocket, and then—' He stopped, hesitated, swore and said roughly, 'Come on!'

Morris limped painfully after. And then? *Idiot question,* he thought wearily; there isn't any 'and then'. They might make it to the rocket and they might not; but whatever happened, there was no future for them.

He paused to catch his breath. Apart from the din Cliteman made pounding through the brush ahead, it was quiet in the woods. The blue-white light from Neighbour filtered down through the leaves. There was a sighing, whispering noise behind him that might have been the fire they left, and might have been the wind; he didn't turn his head to look. He didn't even look up at the distant overhead whistling that, beyond doubt, was the sound of midge jets looking for them. They would be hard to spot in the brush – at least until daylight.

Resolutely, he didn't think beyond daylight.

Cliteman was getting pretty far ahead. Morris stood up. He spread his fingers for a moment, and glanced at the little wrecked midge plane. It had been a foolish impulse to pick it up from the sand beside the fire. It might have been safe enough there; the little creatures would have been cooked alive. But were they any safer with him? He glanced at them; they were still moving, at least. Perhaps he should put them on the ground and leave them, he thought...

But he didn't. In a moment he closed his fingers over the tiny ship and limped after Cliteman.

4

Morris was sitting at his instrument board, transmitting the news of their arrival to Earth. He was well fed, well rested, his wounds entirely healed; the Earth signals were coming through, giving landing instructions and congratulations to the whole crew. Things were fine. The only little flaw was that, for some reason, the rocket motors of the ship were coughing explosively, jarring him, making it hard to receive the faint signal from Earth...

'Wake up, Morris!'

He sat up with a start and looked around.

No radio instruments, no ship, no signals from Earth.

He was half propped against a tree, in the woods, and a soft rain was filtering down through the leaves overhead. Sharp coughing explosions were coming from somewhere nearby. The rockets? Then he remembered. No, not rockets. It was midge flyers, dropping their little missile bombs, stabbing into the unseen ground beneath the treetops, trying to connect with Cliteman and himself. None of them were coming very close – but the midges had plenty of bombs.

Morris coughed raspingly and stood up. Cliteman was grumbling, 'It's getting light. Do you see the rocket?'

Morris bent and retrieved the little midge ship. The three occupants were still moving – more weakly, he thought.

Something was glittering, out beyond the fringes of the dense wood. Perhaps a quarter of a mile away, catching light from setting Neighbour, washed out by the beginning glow of Canopus itself.

'Is that it?'

'No, you idiot! Can't you see it's moving?' Cliteman muttered to himself, pacing back and forth, staring out. The younger man was pretty near collapse, Morris judged. That made two of them. He squinted at the glittering thing. It was moving, all right – well, that ruled out the possibility of its being the rocket. But what was it? Something low to the ground and metallic, crawling back and forth in an open stretch. Large, as midge standards went – a yard or more long. Perhaps it was some sort of agricultural machinery, gang-ploughs, sowers, whatever the midges used. The small community where Morris had been a forced labourer had had nothing like it; but, of course, he hadn't seen anything like enough of the midge civilization to judge what technological heights it might attain.

He glanced up, and saw the glimmer of midge jets circling about. The distant cough of the little bombs seemed to come mostly towards the west in the direction of setting Neighbour; and looking at the patterned jets, Morris realized that most of them were over there too. Now, why should they think we're over that way? he wondered.

And then he knew.

'Cliteman! If you were a midge, where would you expect us to head for?'

Cliteman scowled fretfully. 'How the devil do I know? Oh – towards the rocket, I guess. Where else is there?'

'Nowhere else, Cliteman! So – they're probably concentrated around the rocket. And if you'll look at those jets...'

Cliteman looked surprised, then merely worried again. 'You're right, I suppose. Well – let's try that way. God knows we won't be any worse off, even if we don't find it!'

But they did.

They had to pay a price, because the midge jets were thick as wasps about a nest, but in the glimmering, predawn light they saw the looming tail-rockets of their scout towering over the trees that lay between.

They paused for a just a second to catch their breath, then Cliteman bellowed, 'All right, let's get going!' And he lumbered out of the shelter of the woods, Morris limping and scuttling along behind him.

It was a matter of seconds only, and then the midge aircraft had them spotted. *Thank God,* thought Morris with a part of his brain as he ran, *thank God they don't seem to have guns on the jets!* But the little buzzing craft came racing in at them as though they intended to ram, swerving off at the last moment, dropping little rice-grain objects that spun and crashed like tiny firecrackers – but louder and more dangerously than any firecrackers that Morris had ever seen.

Cliteman was roaring and flailing his arms as he ran; perhaps that helped, for the midge jets could have come closer still, and then they would not have missed. As it was they veered away short, and though the tiny bombs made ant craters fly up all about the running feet of the Earthmen, and the pelting sand from the blasts stung their bare flesh, there were no direct hits. The attackers buzzed by in squads and formations and several of them made Morris duck fearfully as, Kamikaze-like, they swooped in directly at his head. That would be no mere wound, the things, small as they were, had the speed and impact of a bullet. But if the pilots had intended to ram, they missed, or changed their minds; and the two men were untouched all the way across the wide sandy field with its fuzzy little growth of midge crops...

And there was the rocket.

'Hurry, hurry!' cried Cliteman over his shoulder, and Morris tried to respond:

For the midges were waiting:

Ranked about the rocket were little squares of midge troops, or police, or whatever it was in the midge race that fired electric cannon at invading Earthmen. Even a dozen yards away, Morris could hear the thin cheeping as the midges caught sight of them and prepared to open fire. *Splat! Splatsplatsplatsplat!* A burst of the searing little sparks clustered about Cliteman's head and shoulders; he roared, for though most had near misses, the one that connected had brought agony with it. He stumbled and half fell against the open port of the rocket. *Splat!* Apparently it was hard for the midge gunners to bring their pieces to bear on a moving target, even so huge a one as an Earthman; for the next burst stained the sides of the rocket itself. Cliteman leaped and struggled and made it inside.

Lurching after him, Morris caught confused pictures of the rocket. There had been changes! Up against the hull of the rocket there was a shiny, spiralling ramp – not to the main port, that the humans used, but to a neat, square-cut hole, burned out of the hull by the looks of it. *Of course, of course,* Morris told himself fretfully, running and dodging and panting, *of course the midges wouldn't have left it alone! Would we have left such a thing alone if it had landed in New York?* No doubt the rocket had swarmed with the little things since the first moment after they landed ...

And what damage they might have done inside Morris didn't bother to speculate. It didn't matter; they couldn't move the rocket, couldn't escape by flying away – and lacking that it didn't matter how terrible a fight they put up, or what weapons they could contrive from the blasters and hand-guns they might find. One of them was more than a million midges in mass, but they were outnumbered not by millions but by billions ...

And then there was no more time for thought.

The midge gunners had found the range, and he was stung by a thousand flaming sparks. Only hand weapons so far, but he had already seen that even the hand weapons could kill. They had killed Fuller, months before, and they might kill him now. He screamed and jolted forward, swerving and bobbling, and if anything saved his life it was the appearance of Cliteman at the door of the rocket, drawing part of the fire. For a moment Morris thought dazedly that Cliteman had come to his rescue, but only for a moment. He saw Cliteman's dancing, convulsing body, and knew that – of course, of course! – there had been midges even inside the rocket, waiting!

But even so – it was better inside the rocket than out. For outside it was plain death.

Morris plunged towards the door as Cliteman was plunging out. They collided and fell.

Morris jolted to the ground, and the breath left him. So this was the end, he thought wearily. Well, let it come ...

But something was nagging at him.

He remembered what he was carrying, what he held in his hand all through the long flight, protecting it, trying to find the right place and the right time to put it down.

The wrecked midge flyer!

The tiny figures inside still moved, he saw, and he was glad. With almost the last of his strength, the maddening blue sparks charring him by inches, he stretched out his hand and opened the fingers, gently – about to set the flyer on the ground.

And then his fingers closed on it again.

Morris sat up, staring at the little machine. Heedless of the scorching fire from the midge weapons, heedless of the doing, singing jets overhead.

The pain no longer mattered. It was a fact of life, and there was nothing he could to about it. He put it out of his mind.

Morris set the midge flyer on the ground. He stood up, raised his huge foot over it, brought it down – fast, hard, brutal...

And stopped. The foot, huge as Cheops' tomb above the little flyer, halted and hovered, while the tiny creatures inside stared up with huge eyes.

Morris pulled back his foot. Slowly, solemnly, he shook his head – '*no*' to the left, '*no*' to the right.

He bent, picked up the flyer again, set it carefully away, and slumped to the ground.

Lord help us, he thought, *Lord help us, that's all I can do...*

And then he closed his eyes, and waited for the pain to end, with the end of all pain that is dying.

But death didn't come.

There was an agony and a fiery burning but not death. It was hard to tell if there were new wounds falling on Morris' ravaged back, or only the endured pain of the old ones. There was pain, all right; but bearable pain – not the cruel, killing pain that Fuller must have felt, that Morris had expected.

He opened his eyes.

The massed weapons of the midges were ranged on him; but they weren't firing.

He looked around. Overhead the midge flyers swooped and whistled; but they weren't dropping their destructive small bombs.

Morris raised himself on his arms, fearing to hope, hoping

for an end to fear. Beside him, Cliteman's incredulous voice said, 'They aren't shooting at us!'

It was true. And there before them both was the answer. The little flyer that Morris had so carefully carried, so carefully set out of harm's way. There was no one in it now; but one tiny midge sat painfully on the ground beside it looking up at them.

If the flat, huge-eyed face wore an expression, Morris couldn't read it. But what he could read beyond question was the fact that the other two were gone – to the midges manning the guns, beyond doubt. Gone to tell them that – that...

'Why, they must have told the others we meant no harm,' whispered Cliteman, and looked wonderingly at Morris.

Morris nodded slowly.

Cliteman pulled himself painfully to his feet. 'Morris the Destroyer,' he breathed, and there was no irony in his tone. 'Morris the Giver of Life. You showed them we didn't want to kill, and they understood.'

He helped Morris to his feet, and the two of them stood regarding the slowly advancing midges, now with their weapons turned to the ground.

'I'm glad,' said Cliteman; 'I'm glad you took such good care of the three in the plane.'

5

Executive Officer Yardsley, favouring his bandaged and splinted arm, squinted at his desk calculator and announced, 'We're in an orbit that'll hold us for a while, I guess. Any word from the landing party?'

'I'll check with the radio room,' said the Officer of the Deck, and dialled its combination on the intercom.

Yardsley leaned back, patting the bandages on his arm. Outside the viewscreen, bright Canopus blazed at them. It had been a rough trip, complicated with hostile inhabitants on the planet of the star called Neighbour. He was entirely ready for the long, peaceful trip back to Earth, as soon as they collected the crew of the scout rocket that had gone down to look over the Canopan planet – it couldn't be too long or too peaceful for Executive Officer Yardsley. He had made the mistake of volunteering for the landing party on the planet that circled Neighbour; and when the aborigines turned out to be large green anthropoids with Stone Age culture and surly tempers, he had been one of those who had been on the receiving end of the slung stones that greeted them.

The OOD was listening with considerable interest to whatever it was the radio room had to report, Yardsley noted. At last he said, 'Good-oh, thanks,' and hung up.

'Well?' demanded Yardsley.

'Oh, they've had a ball,' the OOD told him, grinning. 'The radio room just established contact, and they haven't got the whole story yet. But enough. They had a little trouble at first, but now they've established contact with the native population. Civilized, Yardsley – and they've got machines, aircraft, everything. And, oh, yes – they only average about half an inch high!'

'Half an inch high,' repeated Yardsley, remembering the green anthropoids. He sighed. 'Wouldn't you know it? I had a free choice – I could have gone with them, or I could have landed on Neighbour. Just my luck to pick the one that was *dangerous*.'

MAKING LOVE

As THE END of the month approached, Katzenherr began to be sharp with his maintenance crews and to press his office girls to complete their progress reports for the main office. It was like that every month. The stresses accumulated. Katzenherr, who was a poet as opportunity offered, took pride in his work because it was socially useful, and pleasure because the House was so vast, so beautifully landscaped and so handsomely decorated. But he could not like his customers.

For them he had a sort of fatherly contempt, as for a child who writes a letter to Santa Claus. The child is deceived and foolish, although he does get his gifts, because his father reads the letter. So deceived and foolish were Katzenherr's customers ... and so rewarded.

Katzenherr's title was Project Chief. On the last of the month he abandoned his green steel office and roamed the House, interfering and supplanting. A boss should be able to do the work of any of his subordinates, he thought, and indeed he could. Sometimes he took over the reception room, seeing that the lyserge dispensers were kept filled, making change for the customers, conducting their tranced steps from the waiting-room to the cubicles that, to them were motels or sylvan nooks, as their hallucinated desires dictated. Sometimes he ran the window washer. Sometimes he took a turn in Maintenance, inspecting and replacing the tapes that went into the featureless plastic mannequins they called Chatty Hedy and Chatty Chuck. Sometimes he kept the books, or checked them, and sometimes he took the place of the customer-relations man who sampled reactions from the customers as, sated, fuzzy-smiling and relaxed, they were about to leave the House. Katzenherr was very expert with the customers and did not ever give them any reason to believe that the Venus or Adonis with whom they had just performed the delicate farce of love was only a blob of clay. He did, however, laugh to himself at their joy.

In other moods, at the end of the month or when a failure of scansion made him scowl and snap his thumbs, he detested the patrons of the House. Why should the PCA make him pander to their clumsy animal lust? He could not disguise from himself, in those moments when he faced the truth that he was not an Eliot or a Ciardi, the other truth, that he was a sort of transistorized pimp, keeper of an electronic bawdyhouse. At such times he returned to basic-basic. Major premise: the human animal has a compelling sex drive. Minor premise: the world has too many people to feed. But there was a complicating factor, an intrusion of unruly human drives into the syllogism. Granting the logic, the world's people coupled joyously and forgot the pill, were too impatient for the old fashioned pessary, or – in transports of romantic attachment – actually *wanted* unplanned (and hence unauthorized) children; and all the bedrooms burst and blossomed. Conclusion: forget about the dangers of the sex drive. Find a better way to sate it. Find a something that, as part of the artificial controlling of the total environment, would make each human's sex life a thing of instant perfection.

And the something better was the House where each man created his own subjective perfection. Splendid, thought Katzenherr at this point in his musing. Then, reassured that the work he did was as important in its way as any number of sonnet sequences, he was able to go on with his duties.

Yet he thought the proceedings were ludicrously comic. He could not help it. It was the poet in him, and at month's end it made him irritable as he stalked the hall with the faint sounds of oscillator squeals and ragged breathing from beyond the cubicle doors.

He was not a very good poet, for he was able to intuit

more than his talents would allow him to express, but he did have perception, and he could see the grotesque comedy in the House. The patrons came up the winding path through the trees and flowerbeds and, lulled in part by their surroundings but even more by their own internal wish, allowed themselves to be soothed and deceived still more by the cup of lyserge and the Muzak drone in the waiting-room. Split from the real world, they manufactured a world of their own. He let himself into the waiting-room and looked at their faces. That slim boy in blue walking shorts swallowing his cup of instant schizophrenia. The round-eyed man, already bemused, who fed coins into the dispenser and received the plastic coded key that would activate his Chatty Hedy. He tried to guess from the play of expression on their blurred faces what remembered bedroom they would think themselves entering, what imagined love words the mannequin would hum into their ears. The tapes had only four sounds – a 'white' hiss, as they entered, a five-minute 420-cycle whine for conversation, an ecstatic *eep! eep!* and an infrasonic drone diminishing at the end. It was the mind of the patron that put meaning into the electronic squeal, just as it was his mind that painted features on the caricature of a face and saw landscapes in the abstract play of light on the walls. Love, thought Katzenherr wryly, like beauty, is in the mind of the observer, but he could not help wondering what sorts of love their minds had made, and on impulse he went through the service passage to the exit lounge and waited for the round-eyed man to come out.

It was a failure, as all his previous experiments had been failures. He administered the antidotes for the lyserge and questioned the man closely, but he was disappointed. What the man had had was as meaningless to Katzenherr as intercourse with a Japanese doll. So he returned to his office and fretted. But not for long, because it was the end of the month, and his leave papers and tickets were waiting on his desk. At this time, Katzenherr appreciated his success most of all. As a Project Chief for the Population Control Administration, he possessed the privilege of real love. Not often. Not easily. But once a month he turned his affairs over to his deputy, packed a bag, caught the southbound jet and spent the weekend that made up for all the rest.

An hour after the end of his working day he was airborne. Strain was gone. He sipped a cocktail and stretched, yawned, smiled to himself with an anticipation of delight. At journey's end, his Helen was waiting, beautiful, bright, loving Helen, and he would be with her that night. There, among the pleasant gardens where she lived, bringing her his gift of violets from the dispenser outside her door, Katzenherr would expend his budget of rapture. He was too contented to despise, but he could not help feeling a gentle contempt for the patrons of his House, who would live out their lives gulled by an electronic sham and never know true delights of love.

Any more than would he.

WAY UP YONDER

THE THIN LITTLE voice buzzed and sang: 'Good morning, Sutherland Master! Good morning, Boss.'

Berl Sutherland jumped with all his arms and legs at once, like a startled infant, and awoke.

He was in a canopied bed, in – yes, he remembered now – in the Old House of the Blick plantation. The maid was fussing around him.

'This is Persephone,' cooed the maid's voice. 'I am your personal servant, Sutherland Master. The colonel wishes you good morning and hopes you enjoy your stay.'

'Thanks,' said Sutherland blurrily.

It was all beginning to come back to him – the long flight from Leesville, the arrival in the middle of the night, the sister of the girl he loved, who had made him welcome.

He watched the maid, bending over him, setting something down on the night table, touching the buttons that opened the shades and turned on the air vents and brought gently brisk music out of the speaker grille beside his bed. They certainly took care of their company on these plantations, he thought in sleepy admiration.

He sat up reluctantly.

'You wish to rise now, Sutherland Master?' The maid's voice came from under his pillow. That puzzled Sutherland for a moment; he had been on the planet less than twenty-four hours and its customs were still unfamiliar to him.

'Yeah, I wish to rise,' he replied.

The maid said, 'Your clothes are laid out. Call if you wish me, Sutherland Master. The name is Persephone.'

'Thanks,' said Sutherland, but only to air; the maid had buzzed through the room at high speed and was gone.

He shrugged and got out of bed.

It was a nice room, too, he thought with a touch of worry. The bed had a handsome spread of gold brocade, now neatly folded down; the carpeting was thick, the furniture expensive. Thelma's family really had it.

What in all the worlds, he wondered, did she see in him? Sutherland wasn't used to underrating himself; he was aware that he was young, healthy, reasonably bright. But he was also aware that his draft number was up and that his total income for the year would hardly buy the contents of this one room, let alone the enormous rest of the plantation owned by Colonel Blick, Thelma's brother. Still...

Well, she had invited him here. Too bad she couldn't have been on hand when he arrived, but there it was.

Sutherland got up, staggered over to the window and, wincing, tried to draw the shades again. Sunlight was all right in its place, but what was coming in the window was a sallow orange colour, and brighter than he liked even so. But there seemed to be no way for him to draw the shades. The maid had pushed a button, he remembered, but which one?

To Sutherland's groggy inspection, there seemed to be at least fifty – if all the round, square and toggle-shaped things on the control panel by the bed could be called buttons – and which of them might control the windows, he had no idea.

Nor, on second thought, did he want to tempt fate by experimenting. It was all getting very complicated, he thought worriedly. It hadn't seemed a bit complicated back on Earth, where one normal bright moon had filled one normal starlit sky, and one extremely normal girl named Thelma Coolidge Blick had been out on the balcony with him. But that was half a year ago, and a good many light-years away, and besides there hadn't been a war on then. Now he was on Lee, sixth planet of the larger component of Sirius, and Thelma was – where *was* Thelma?

'Excuse me, sir,' said a timid voice.

Sutherland jumped. In the doorway of the bath – *his* bath – stood a small dark man. And in his hand the man held, for the Lord's sake, a mint julep.

The man coughed apologetically. 'I am Miguel Mookerjan, your neighbour. Pardon this intrusion.'

'Good morning,' growled Sutherland.

'Yes,' said Mookerjan thoughtfully, 'I suppose it is.' He inspected the room, coming at last to the glass in his hand. 'Oh, yes. Perhaps you would care for this? I am a Muslim,' he said with pride, 'and we are not allowed alcohol. But I do not wish to offend our host. So I came through the bath which we share to offer you, as you might perhaps say, a dividend.'

Sutherland was puzzled, but he followed the direction of Mookerjan's eyes, and the answer to his puzzlement was on the table by his bed. A mint julep; the maid had brought him one of the confounded things too. Before breakfast!

'But you have not drunk your own,' said Mookerjan with concern. 'You are not of the Faith? Or perhaps AA? Or – oh, I see. I deduce, sir ...'

'Berl Sutherland.'

'I deduce, Mr Sutherland, that you have never visited the colonel before?'

Sutherland shook his head.

'Ah, yes. I suppose,' said Mookerjan thoughtfully, 'that you are a business associate? A buyer of proto-spuds for one of the interplanetary exchanges? No? Then perhaps an attorney – I have heard that there are some estate matters to be settled. Or could you have known his father, the late Colonel Blick, or are you related in family? Or ...'

'Mr Mookerjan,' said Sutherland dangerously, 'I'll tell you my business here without your dredging for it. I'm engaged to be married to his sister.'

'Oh, splendid!' cried Mookerjan. 'A wonderful girl, Mr Sutherland! I assure you, I have met many charming young ladies, but few compare with Robin Blick!'

'*Thelma* Blick, Mr Mookerjan.'

'That sister? But—' Mookerjan hesitated. 'Well,' he said,

'I wish you every happiness. And now I imagine you wish to dress. You will not want to be late for breakfast. The colonel is *so* much more approachable then! *A bientôt,* Mr Sutherland, *à bientôt!*'

The Blick place was nothing special for the planets of the Sirian system. Sparsely populated, rich and fertile, the Sirian planets spawned countless thousands of aristocrats, so the colonel was by no means exceptional. But the total effect of the big house, seen by day, was enough to dwindle what remained of the morale of Berl Sutherland.

Discount the wide marble staircase that wound down from the sleeping floor to the great hall at the entrance. Don't consider the obvious wealth of the furnishings – tapestried walls and finely made furniture, all of them imported across light-years of space at a shipping cost Sutherland could not guess. These could be hand-me-downs; the antebellum South on Earth, centuries before, owned many such a plantation where the owners counted themselves lucky to see a hundred dollars in cash from one year to the next.

But there was much more – *so* much more. The food. The fine liquors. And, over and above everything else, the servants.

To Sutherland's bewildered eye, there seemed to be more servants than people in the room. All the same size, all the same shape, all stamped out of the same dies in the same factories. The plantations of Lee had their slaves, and the slaves were robots; they moved about the rooms of the Blick plantation house like busy beetles, cleaning, removing, serving and tending.

Degenerate, thought Sutherland angrily. You certainly wouldn't know there was a war on. Why must these people act like Confederate massas? A body servant for every guest and the most personal tasks done for you – it was revolting; it was nothing like the stripped-down, Spartan life he had been brought up to on Earth...

But it just might be, he thought, that if there had been

an endless labour supply available on Earth, every human might have just such a home. Meanwhile, he was here. He would, he decided, attempt to enjoy it.

'Good morning,' he said to the room at large, and let a small bronze-coloured servant take him to a chair. Thelma was not in sight, he had noted at once, which freed him to observe the others who were.

The Blicks liked a house full. Lolling against the upholstered pillar of a round divan, Colonel Blick himself was reading the paper and answering absently the remarks of his guests. He had nodded to Sutherland, nothing more. Miguel Mookerjan glanced up, smiled emptily, and returned to his meal. The others gave Sutherland scarcely that much attention. All right, thought Sutherland belligerently, who the devil do you think you are?

But he remembered that his plan was to enjoy himself, and he gestured to the servants wheeling the little tables of food.

Neither of the Blick sisters was in the room. There were three young men, a matched set, wearing the same informal sort of uniform as Colonel Blick; like him, they were more interested in their newspapers than in human society. There were a couple of girls whose identity Sutherland couldn't guess, and a man in dark glasses on Sutherland's left, solemnly eating, like a stoker filling a furnace, without looking up.

And then Thelma floated into the room.

Sutherland stood up hastily. 'Darling!' she cried across sixty feet of wall-to-wall carpeting. 'Dearest, I'm *so* glad you got here! I've been counting the minutes!'

Sutherland said awkwardly, 'Hello, dear.' Why, he thought, astonished, this is a beautiful girl. She was blonde, heavy-haired blonde, with two solid coils spiralling away from the nape of her neck; her eyes were bluest blue, her figure perfect.

'You know Robin,' she said kindly, standing on tiptoe to be kissed.

There was another girl with her – the sister, the one who had let him in. Sutherland nodded.

'Poor angel,' said Thelma softly, 'I know what's bothering you. You wanted me to be here when you arrived.'

'Not necessarily,' said Sutherland quickly, 'but...'

'But I couldn't. Of course I couldn't! Aren't you sweet to understand that? And I *would* have been there, dearest, if it hadn't been for that terrible party at the Grossfaders last night. And when Pat Grossfader brought me home and I heard that you'd arrived and gone to bed, why, I just wanted to *throw* myself into your arms. And I would have, too, if I hadn't been the *teeniest* bit high. Oh, those sloe gin daiquiris!'

'I hope you had a pleasant night's sleep,' the mousy sister said more formally to Sutherland.

He nodded again. 'Fine, thanks.'

Across the room, Colonel Blick was reading something from the paper, laughing. Sutherland allowed the servant to help him to kippers, scrambled eggs, yogurt and a blend of eight kinds of fruit juices sweetened with Antarean honey.

'Try the toast,' Robin Blick said politely. 'It's our own bread, baked from the proto-spuds we grow.'

'I'm not very hungry,' Sutherland apologized. He was craning his neck. Odd, but while the robots were serving him, Thelma seemed to have disappeared. 'I wonder...'

Robin said, 'She's probably in the butler's pantry. She'll be back.'

Sutherland felt a faint chill. Around the room, the conversation flowed smoothly. Mr Mookerjan was inquiring nervously about the animal origins of his fried scrapple. The three young army officers were chattering about the shootin' and fishin' on every landable planet in five solar systems. The girls – Thelma had brought them home from the party at the Grossfaders, it turned out – were perkily comparing hangovers.

'I think,' said Sutherland apologetically, 'that I'd like to talk to your brother.'

'Sure,' said Robin Blick. 'Help yourself.'

Getting up, Sutherland made his way across the room. The colonel was deep in his newspaper, preening his beard. It was a hard beard to preen, being pale gold in colour and the texture of the down on the back of a new-hatched chick. The colonel was nineteen years old.

'Oh, hello there,' said the colonel, looking up for a moment, and 'Damn! Charles did you see this in the paper? Grogan's going back to Mars.'

'Mars!' cried the nearest of the young officers, dashed. 'Good heavens! But he promised to come here!'

The other youths joined the chorus. Sutherland listened, puzzled. Whoever this Grogan was, he was somebody important. Perhaps a crop buyer, he thought; he knew that the big combines on Earth sent their representatives around. Or – well, it could be something more important, something to do with the war.

'I don't remember the name,' he said politely. 'Is Grogan a commission buyer?'

'Commission buyer—' The colonel put his paper down and looked at Sutherland more carefully. 'My dear fellow, Grogan's a musician.'

'A roar-and-shack soarer, friend,' said Charles.

'Oh, that roar!' added the second of the other officers.

'And that shack!'

'Come along!' cried the colonel, jumping up. 'You've got to hear his latest tape, Sutherland!'

And that was that, as far as talking to the boy about anything as important as his sister's hand was concerned; Sutherland couldn't get his attention that long.

He sat listening to the subtly buzzing drone of roar-and-shack music as long as he could take it, but that wasn't very long, and when he escaped and looked for Thelma, she was gone.

'Women's business,' she had said, according to her sister Robin, but what the women's business was, Thelma had not said and Robin did not choose to tell.

Ho-hum, thought Sutherland, somewhat dampened, it isn't a bit the way it looked from that balcony on Earth.

2

The man in the dark glasses said, 'I suppose you'll be going in, eh? Good luck, Sutherland. I was in the last one.'

Sutherland was impressed. Overhead, the orange-tinted plastic dome let in enough of the light from blazing bright Sirius to bring the intensity to Earth standards though the hues were all blue-white or dying under the unshielded ultra-violet.

Sutherland looked sidelong at the man in the dark glasses, his face sallow in the orange light, and said, 'I guess it was pretty rough.'

'Oh, rough enough,' the man said modestly. His name was LaFargue and he was only five years or so older than Sutherland. He must have lied about his age, Sutherland thought abstractedly. 'The worst thing is that you never see the enemy. Interstellar war isn't personal. It's chart your line of fire and pop your missiles off and wait. Well, it takes forty days to get to the nearest star even in subspace, you know. But it takes four *years* for the light to come back, so you don't know what luck you're having.'

'But then how do you know ...'

'You don't know. You don't know a thing, not until the peace is declared and you can fly out there and look. We got two planets of the Antarean system, they tell me. I guess the light ought to be hitting Earth any day now. But I never went and looked. Didn't want to.' He nodded politely and went back to the house.

Sutherland continued to stroll around the gardens. That was a good war, he thought, when we fought the Antareans. Six months of hard fighting and it was all over; they got Pluto and two of Jupiter's outer moons, but who cared about those? Only there was always the chance that a missile might hit a really important planet. Mars, say, with its fifty million souls. Venus, with its quarter-billion. Or – Earth.

He swallowed, thinking of what an interstellar missile might do to rabbit-warren Earth.

For that matter, war could well come to this planet – yes, to Lee, to the whole Sirian system. It was the technique of interstellar war to stand back and try to batter your enemy to pieces, but that technique was predicated on the sure assumption that your enemy would pulverize any fleet you might send against him.

That assumption held good for Antares, for Sol, for the present enemy system of Capella – but Sirius, after all, was a frontier system. There were a few space corvettes, a few emplacements on the smaller satellites, nothing that would give a flotilla of dreadnaughts any serious opposition. The Sirian system was fat and open to the war's dangers...

Assuming, of course, that the Sirian system was really *in* the war. Sutherland couldn't help feeling that war was strangely remote here. No one seemed to *care*.

Still, the Sirian system was certainly important to the war – from Earth's point of view, anyhow.

Lee was only one of the three habitable planets, but it was a good one. It produced food enough for fifty times its own population, food that Earth could very well use.

The planet was near enough to its immense primary for the rays to be deadly to all who faced it without protection. That was why the plantation houses were shielded, why the crops were worked by robots. Humans wouldn't do. They would die.

Still, thought Sutherland remotely, *he* would rather have human beings around him than...

He jumped as a shadow crossed his face.

It was one of the robots, holding something out to him. 'Curse you,' snapped Sutherland, 'what do you mean sneaking up on me like that?' He was startled, and surprise brought on anger.

The servant, silent as a shadow, continued mutely to offer him the thing that was in its hands. Sutherland looked at it at last and recognized it: a small shoulder radio.

'Oh,' said Sutherland ungraciously. 'Thanks. I—' He stopped, remembering. He strapped the radio on and turned on the switch. 'Thanks,' he said again knowing that this time the robot would hear.

'You are welcome, Sutherland Massa,' said the robot's unhurried uninflected voice. 'Is there anything you wish?'

'No' – he looked at the robot's chest – 'no, Persephone.' Yes, that was the same one that had brought him his morning julep, his own personal attendant. The name was inscribed on its torso plates. 'You can go,' he said, and watched the little thing move silently away.

'Mr Sutherland,' said a girl's voice from behind him, 'you really ought to keep your radio on. It's unsettling to the servants.'

'Sorry.' It was Thelma's mousy sister, Robin. 'I try to remember,' he said, with only part truth. The servants were robots, same as the field hands, and their voices were radio, not sound – as their 'eyes' were radar instead of receptors for the visual spectrum of light. In order for them to hear or be heard, they needed radio equipment. That was the little box – the same little box he had slept with under his pillow.

'The gardens are lovely this morning,' Robin Blick said flatly, nodding, and prepared to move away.

Sutherland was galvanized into action. 'Oh, Miss Blick. I wonder if you can tell me where the colonel is.'

The girl stopped and looked at him more thoughtfully.

'I want to – uh – see him,' Sutherland explained.

She nodded.

'I want to talk to him about – about something.'

'Yes,' she said, and smiled. Smiling, she wasn't mousy at all. 'I thought you wanted to talk to him about something.'

That was very pleasing, Sutherland decided; he couldn't help grinning. 'Oh,' he said, relaxing, 'then Thelma's said something to you? Of course. Why shouldn't she? Sisters are always close, exchanging confidences and so on.'

He looked around the garden hastily. There, in a patch of portulaca, was a marble bench. 'I tell you, Miss Blick – Robin. Won't you sit down for a minute? I've got a few things that are – well, worrying me.'

'I bet you have,' said Robin Blick. But she let him lead her to the bench.

She didn't look a bit like her sister – brown hair, brown eyes, a figure that was nice enough but hardly startling, and Thelma was definitely startling. But Robin seemed, thought Berl Sutherland, a friendly, sisterly sort of girl, who might be just the person to clear up the one or two little doubts that in the last twelve hours had percolated up to the surface of his mind.

'The thing,' he said, 'is that Thelma's such a high-spirited young creature. I wonder if she's *ready* for marriage. I thought I might have a chance to discuss it with your brother, but he seems rather...'

'My brother,' said Robin Blick clearly, 'is a flat-headed halfwit. He's only nineteen years old and maybe he'll smarten up – some. But he's got a long way to go.'

'I see,' said Sutherland after a second. 'I only thought that – you know, head of the family, good manners, the right thing to do, all that sort of thing.'

'I am sick to my stomach of that sort of thing, Mr Sutherland,' said Robin Blick in a pleasantly conversational tone. 'I am sick to death of Lee and everything about it.'

Sutherland cleared his throat. Things were getting out of hand; it was time to get the conversation back where he wanted it.

He said, 'Tell me, what did Thelma say about me when she told you? I mean if it isn't a secret.'

'It isn't a secret. She didn't say a word.'

'But...'

'She didn't even say you were coming, young man.'

Sutherland bristled. Young man, indeed! Surely the girl was younger than he!

'But I thought you said you had an idea what I wanted.'

'Mr Sutherland,' said Robin Blick patiently, 'I've been Thelma's sister for a long time now. You mustn't think you're the first young man who's come to talk to her brother.'

Sutherland followed Robin Blick on a guided tour through the gardens, but it was wasted on him. His thoughts were of Thelma Blick and not of the place in which he found himself for the love of her.

But it was an interesting place, all the same.

The dome around the Blick manor house was a quarter of a mile across. Nearly thirty acres bloomed under its shallow orange roof. There was the house itself and its gardens. There were six acres of farm, for the beets and tomatoes and crisp green lettuce that did poorly in Sirius' direct light. There was an artificial pond, three acres of it, that stocked fine smallmouths and doubled as a reservoir in case of fire. There was a grove of fruit trees, and there were a dozen acres of pasture for the colonel's select herd of registered Black Angus.

Of course, that was only the domed portion of the estate. Outside the dome, naked under the blue violence of the primary, were over two hundred square miles. It was more than a plantation, more than a Texan's ranch; it was a principality.

This was the thing about Lee's perfect climate: no dust. There wasn't any, the result of high ionization from the rays of the primary; the dust clumped and agglutinated and fell. Well, there was a *little* – if there had been none, that would have been the end of farming, because it would have been the end of rain. Water vapour cannot coalesce readily without tiny dust granules for each droplet to form around. But because there was some dust, though not a great deal, the water vapour formed itself in large drops, fell and washed the air clean. Result: enough rain, and very small and few clouds between times. A perfect growing climate.

And the crops that were grown were something very special indeed. The name of the principal crop was protospuds. A miracle crop!

Wrench off the tops and you can cook yourself a superb mess of greens, rich in vitamins A, C, D and a dozen others. Dig the tuberous root and it is a treasure of assorted food.

The peel, toasted, has a fine nutlike flavour that bakes into delectable bread. Pulled young and green and cooked whole, the tubers resemble a super-Jerusalem artichoke.

If none of these makes a dish to your liking, let the whole thing go to flower and seed. Then the petals make a splendid jam, a first-rate source of all the B vitamins. The seeds, toasted, split into hulls and kernels. The hulls become a peppery spice, the seeds a richly perfumed sort of cinnamon.

It was a valued crop and – variously cooked, dried, radio-sterilized or frozen – it made a priceless export article for interstellar trade, and an essential part of production for war.

All of this Berl Sutherland listened to, or seemed to, but not much of it stayed with him.

'There is one thing,' he said at last, when Robin Blick paused and looked at him and seemed to expect a question. 'I mean there's something I'd like to know. Wasn't – wasn't Thelma *sincere* back on Earth?'

'You'll have to ask her yourself,' said Robin, sighing, because he was a very nice boy, good-looking and smart and with just the right degree of shyness, and she didn't like what lay ahead for him.

3

It was time for the ten o'clock news. Sutherland fumblingly tried to turn the set on, but a servant shot past him and expertly dialled. In the gun room down the hall, roar-and-shack music whined and thumped.

Sutherland said 'Thanks,' remembered that once again he'd forgotten to turn his radio on, and decided that he didn't care.

Mr Mookerjan drifted over and joined him. 'The war, eh? Good. Let's see how long we have to dance in the citadel while the Red Death roams outside.'

Sutherland glanced at him quickly, but Mookerjan's pale-olive face was pleasantly blank.

The programme was in stereo colour and the timing was perfect; the animated commercial was just ending and the news commentator appeared, picking up his wand and pointing to a wall map.

A fleet action had been fought off Way Rock – though why anyone should fight for a Moon-sized hunk of frozen slag a light-year and a half from any warming star was more than Sutherland could imagine. There was, of course, no victory; the ships had shot at each other for a while, then lost contact in hyperspace evasive action. More than eight hundred planet-smashers had been launched at the enemy in the previous twenty-four hours. It was expected that the first enemy missiles would start exploding at various points in the Sol system within two weeks.

The commentator at that point disappeared, though his voice remained, as the vision tank filled with a perspective star map, all the stellar bodies bright dots of light in flashing colour.

Colonel Blick bawled from the gun room, 'What's all the racket in there? We can't hear ourselves think!'

Self-consciously, Berl Sutherland switched off the set. Colonel Blick appeared, tugging fretfully at his soft pale beard.

'Sorry,' he grumbled, 'but *really!* That's Grogan's latest we were playing and you know how distracting it is to hear a lot of jibber-jabber when he's roaring.'

'Of course,' said Sutherland. He wasn't a roar-and-shacker, but he knew that the idea was that the music itself was supposed to be formless, empty; it was the listener himself who filled in the meaning.

'Kept thinking it was a damn John Philip Sousa March,' complained the colonel. 'Fine thing! Confounded war makes enough trouble. I don't want it busting into my music!'

'I'm sorry,' said Sutherland. This was, after all, Thelma's brother and the head of the family. 'The set's off. You can go ahead with your tape if you want to.'

The colonel threw himself into a chair, breathing hard.

'Later,' he said. 'Oh, that roar! You'll have to come and hear it for yourself, Sutherland. But let me get my breath first. Grogan takes a lot out of you, you know. There's plenty of them that can put out a dull beat, but for real *emptiness* there's nobody like Grogan.'

Sutherland looked quickly around the room, remembering.

It was the first chance he'd had to talk to the colonel, but it was a fine chance; Blick was sitting there and no one else was talking. Mookerjan had picked up a magazine, and apart from him there seemed no possibility of interruption.

Sutherland cleared his throat.

'Sir,' he began, choked on it – the colonel was only nineteen years old, after all! 'Colonel, that is, I've been wanting a word with you.'

'Shoot, man. Roar away.'

'Back on Earth,' Sutherland said rapidly, 'I knew your sister in school. Well, we were drawn to each other. She's a wonderful girl, Colonel Blick, and...'

'Say,' said Blick, sitting up, 'where *is* Thelma? You know, Mookerjan?'

The olive-coloured man looked up from his magazine long enough to shake his head.

'Robin!' Across the room, the elder sister turned around. 'You seen Thelma?'

'She isn't back yet,' Robin Blick called.

'Damn it all,' complained the colonel, sinking back, 'I wish she'd stay around the house long enough to tell me what to do about Pat Grossfader. You're a friend of hers, Mr Sutherland – maybe you can talk to her. Here she's supposed to marry Pat next month, and she's out alley-catting with every man under the age of ninety on Lee. Pat's not going to let her get away with that forever, Sutherland.'

'Supposed,' repeated Sutherland carefully, the words chipping out of his mouth like bits of ice, 'supposed to – to *marry*...?'

'He's put up with plenty from her already,' growled the

colonel, tugging fretfully at his beard. 'I wouldn't blame him if he called the whole thing off! That Mancini boy. That wasn't bad enough. Or the time she and George Henry Twyfort ran out of rocket fuel and stayed in orbit all night.'

Sutherland said, with an expensive effort to make it sound calm and clear: 'You say Thelma's going to ma— to ma...'

'And the trouble is, Sutherland, it's *important*. Pat's land is right next to ours. We have to think about the next generation.'

'Sure you do,' said Sutherland at once, without the faintest idea what he was agreeing to. His mind was suddenly stopped dead in its tracks; it refused to move past the word 'marry'.

'I suppose,' said the colonel reflectively, 'that Pat wouldn't kick up too much of a fuss about Twyfort if it wasn't that the boy thinks Thelma's going to marry him. That'll shack you! Marry him, and he doesn't have a foot of land to call his own!'

'I think,' Sutherland said carefully, 'that I'll just take a little stroll around the grounds.'

He got up and staggered off. The colonel stared after him, then shrugged.

'Nice fellow,' he said to Miguel Mookerjan. 'Wonder why Thelma invited him here.'

In a wing chair before the fire, Sutherland hardly heard the others come into the gun room, and they didn't notice him. That was fine – he had a good deal of fire-staring to do. *Married!*

Dimly, he heard the voice of the colonel, enthusiastically piping, 'You'll like this, LaFargue. *Music to Feel By*. Oh, that Grogan!'

A click and a whir of reels, and a bagpipe drone snarled out of the multiphonic speakers spotted around the walls of the gun room. Curse their nonsense, Sutherland mumbled to himself; but it was easier to stay there and listen than to get up and move. And once he gave the music a chance to work on him, it had something.

Drone, drone; no, it wasn't like a bagpipe, or at least not like the skirling bagpipe melodies. It had only enough variation of pitch to suggest that it was music and not a distant fire siren. It made him think of something. Sutherland thought drowsily, of – of weddings? Yes. Certainly there was a touch of Mendelssohn right there – or something that might have suggested something that was Mendelssohn. Weddings, and bridesmaids in pink and yellow, and Thelma down the aisle, dewy and delightful, and himself in a starchy collar and striped pants...

He caught himself. But he began to see just what it was the fans liked about roar-and-shack.

When the spinning tape-end had *flick-flick-flicked* itself to a stop, Sutherland was feeling relatively good. Well, that was what roar-and-shack was for, too. It brought what was inside you out to the surface, where you could get at it and handle it.

He listened, hardly thinking of Thelma at all, to Colonel Blick's breathless, 'Roar, man, roar! Oh, what a lip that Grogan has!'

'Very nice,' said LaFargue's voice. 'A touch classical, wouldn't you say? Beethoven's Sixth – green fields and a gathering storm, all that sort of thing. And' – the voice became measurably brisker – 'that's what I want to talk to you about, Blick.'

'Eh?'

'There's a storm gathering. Don't you know you're right in the middle of it?'

'Oh, Sam,' protested the colonel's voice with faint indignation. 'Did you come here to nag me about that shortage again? I know there's a war on.'

'You don't act it,' said LaFargue in a cold, scolding tone. 'You plantation colonels act as though the universe was staked down to bedrock. Nothing's going to change, is that it? The way Daddy did things is fine, because everything's always going to be the same as it was in Daddy's day.'

Colonel Blick sighed wistfully. 'I've got a couple of other Grogans here,' he offered, but not as though he thought LaFargue would take him up on it.

'No! Why can't you get the crops out?'

Silence, except for the colonel's sad breathing.

'I'll tell you why,' said LaFargue. 'There isn't a plantation on Lee that's met its quota for three months. Crops rot in the fields. Spuds spoil in storage. The robots aren't doing the job, Blick. It's up to you plantation colonels to get out there and straighten them out.'

'Mr LaFargue!'

'Or would you rather,' LaFargue inquired, 'let the Capellans march in and do it for you? Because if Lee doesn't meet its quotas, Earth isn't going to be able to eat, let alone feed its fighting men.'

'Oh, damn it,' cried the colonel, 'it isn't only *us*, you know.'

'I know. That's the bad part. Pershing's iron mines report one breakdown after another. In the Aldebaranian system, all the remote-operated planets are getting out of hand. I don't know, Blick, maybe we're getting too soft; maybe we've given the robots more than they can handle. But it's up to us humans to step in and set things straight. I'm telling you this for your own good. If you colonels don't do it voluntarily, the government's going to have to step in.'

Colonel Blick said frostily, 'Thank you for your comments, Mr LaFargue. Is there anything else? No? Then, with your permission, I'll return to my other guests.'

Robin Blick looked in the gun room and said: 'Oh, there you are. We've been looking for you.'

Sutherland leaned forward, recovered himself, blinked and set down the glass. 'We?'

'The servants helped me,' Robin said impatiently, taking in the glass and the low-water mark on the brandy decanter. 'You can go now,' she said into the microphone on her shoulder set. 'Mr Sutherland's here.'

There were half a dozen robots with her, Sutherland saw

blurrily. Confounded things, he thought, he wished they looked more like *people*. Or less. They were all of a pattern; only the colouring of the enamel on their faces and torsos distinguished them – that and the name that was neatly lettered across each chest. There was a purple-and-white-checked Vespasian and a blue-polka-dot Theseus, a Ganymede in shades of brown and tan, an Echo in green.

'I thought,' said Robin, distracting him from the reteating robots, 'that you'd like to know that Thelma's back.'

'Oh, fine,' said Sutherland, frowning.

'My *sister*.'

'Oh, *that* Thelma,' said Sutherland agreeably, and stood up. 'Well. Let's go see that Thelma,' he said, taking her arm.

For some reason, this mousy girl named Robin seemed to be impatient with him, Sutherland noticed. That was most annoying of her. If she couldn't be a lady and polite to her guests, then what the devil kind of family was this anyway? A music-mad teenager posing as the head of the household, a rude old maid of every bit of twenty-three bossing the company around, and a faithless, heartless...

'Are you all right, Mr Sutherland?'

'Fine,' he said emptily.

'I thought I heard you grunt or something.'

'I'm fine,' he insisted. 'That's what I said, isn't it? Now where's Thelma?'

They were back in the great manorial hall and the colonel was holding forth. Not on Grogan and his meltingly empty horn this time, but on Lee and its place in the war effort.

'The mother planet,' he was saying pontifically, 'has nothing to fear. We'll do our part! No Earthman will go hungry in this war.'

LaFargue, keeping an obviously tight rein on his tongue, said briefly: 'And if the Capellans occupy you?'

'Occupy?' repeated the colonel, stupefied and staring. '*Occupy* us? The *Capellans*?' And he burst out laughing. 'Oh, very amusing, LaFargue. What do you think of that, friends? *Lee occupied!*'

Even Mr Mookerjan giggled shrilly. LaFargue said doggedly, 'It's not impossible.'

Somebody spoke Sutherland's name, but he wasn't interested. He'd heard the same talk, between the same two men, an hour earlier, and wasn't interested in the recap. What he was interested in was Thelma.

He said, 'Where is she? Thelma, I mean.'

Everyone turned and looked at him. Mr Mookerjan giggled again. 'Why, I saw her out on the terrace with...'

'She *stepped out*,' said Robin, hard and fast, catching an expression on her brother's face. 'She'll be back, Mr Sutherland, so why don't you sit down and have a drink?'

Sutherland blinked. 'Terrace, eh? Well,' he said raising his voice, 'I just feel the need of a little fresh air myself, and what do you think of that?'

The nerve, he told himself aggrievedly, of these frontier-planet civilians, trying to pull the wool over his eyes. Yes, civilians! 'Colonel' was only a courtesy title that went along with inheriting the plantation. What did young Blick or his pasty-faced friends know about war? From his towering seniority as an almost-sworn-in, soon-to-be-inducted draftee, Sutherland looked down on them with irritation and contempt, and he marched across the room and out of the french windows.

'Thelma!' he shouted.

The terrace was empty. Not even their intelligence was any good, he told himself, grieving.

'Thelma!' he cried again, and walked out into the gardens.

'Thelma!' he roared, and circled the little pond, and then he saw her. Or them.

'Oh, you rat!' said Sutherland, and hurled himself at the man with his arms around the woman Sutherland loved. 'I don't care how much money you've got, Pat Grossfader – Thelma loves me and she isn't going to marry you!'

'Wait, buddy!' The man dodged away from the flailing fists. 'Hey! You've got the wrong man! I'm Charley Pough, from Cornell! I never saw Miss Blick before tonight!'

Sutherland said, 'You cad!' He looked at the smeared lipstick and the disarrayed hair of Thelma Blick. 'Hussy!' he cried. 'Faithless woman! You aren't even true to Pat Grossfader, let alone me!'

And he wandered off into the night.

4

Overhead, the unfamiliar constellations twinkled, dim and orange-hued through the canopy. It was full dark. The evening rain had already come and gone; now the fertile ground would steep in moisture until the morning, when bright Sirius would pour its heat and light into the making of another five inches of stalk, another quarter-inch of girth of tuber, of each plant on the Blick place.

Sutherland wandered until something moved in the shadows in front of him.

He jumped. 'Who's there?'

No answer.

'Speak up!' he barked, and then he remembered what he was always forgetting, and touched the switch of the speaker at his shoulder.

'Who's there?' he demanded again, and now the radio received and relayed his voice.

'Apollonius, please, Sutherland Master,' whispered the speaker on his shoulder softly, and a green-and-white-striped robot stood before him, scanning him with its great silver radar eyes. 'Are you lost, Sutherland Master?'

'Lost and damned forever,' groaned Sutherland.

'Do you want Apollonius to take you to the house?' whispered the radio voice, soft and sexless.

'No, damn you.' Ugly wretched little thing. 'Get out of here. Leave me alone!'

'Yes, Sutherland Master.' The four-foot mannikin obediently wheeled and disappeared.

Good, thought Sutherland sourly, glowering after it in the dark – can't stand the things.

Still, he thought, he might as well go back to the house. Faithless woman! But he couldn't stand out here all night. No, back to the house and up to his room. There was a lock on the door; he would use it. Speak to no one. Ignore the whole confounded mass of them. Then up early the next morning, get one of the servants to drive him to town, catch a plane to the spaceport and...

Say, he thought drearily, staring around at the trees, just where *was* the house?

He called uncomfortably, 'Hey, Apollonius, or whatever your name is!'

There wasn't any answer.

'Oh, damn,' said Sutherland, irritated, and snapped the switch off. Never mind the robots; they were as obnoxious as their owners. It was impossible to be lost, he reassured himself – that is, *really* lost. True, he didn't know where he was, but that was only a detail. All he had to do was to go in one direction and keep right on going. Any direction – the way out of a wood is straight ahead, and once he was outside, he'd see the house or the dome, and either would orient him.

The robot had gone *that* way. Well, it was as good a way as any. Sutherland trudged after.

In a moment, he saw where the robot had been heading, and it wasn't towards the house at all. It was an entrance to the servants' quarters underground. It wasn't lighted and there was no one in sight, but it was perfectly clear in the dim orangey glow from the overhead stars.

Sutherland hesitated. 'Apollonius,' he called weakly, but there wasn't any answer.

Undoubtedly, he thought, the tunnel through the servants' quarters was the quickest way back to the house.

The tunnel was dark – more than dark; it was absolute blackness. He could form no idea of its height or length. He hesitated for a while, the drink receding inside him, wondering whether, after all, it was such a good idea to entrust himself to an unknown pit whose only inhabitants would be hateful animalcules.

But the drink was not all gone, and Sutherland didn't care. If Thelma was lost to him, what had life to offer?

Resting one hand against a wall, he carefully advanced. In a dozen paces, he was completely blind, but he remembered his cigarette lighter; flicked it on, found the tunnel was perfectly plain and empty; flicked it off and marched confidently ahead.

Strange sounds stopped him.

Funny, thought Sutherland, was it an army marching at route step or a dance troupe? More than either of those, it was like the irregular crash of raindrops on the sodden fabric of a tent, a sound without timbre, only a multiplied *pat-a-pat-a-pat*. He moved a few yards farther until the noises were close at hand; then flicked on the lighter once more.

In the tiny flare, he saw a serpentine circle of shining bodies. Robots – the house and garden robots, and they were – why, dancing!

Dancing!

They circled about a chamber of the underground quarters and processing works, circled, spun, slipped and slithered in and out of a queerly limited pattern, like cod flopping about in a fisherman's basket. Their silvery radar orbs rolled endlessly. Their linked metal limbs waved and clutched.

Dancing, thought Sutherland, dazed – no one told me robots danced.

It could have been the rain dance of chrome-plated Indian children. It could have been the sacrificial rites of some island cannibals. But it lacked one human attribute that made it very strange indeed.

It was silent.

No music; none at all. There wasn't the thumping of a gasoline-tin drum, or the shrill of a reed fife; there wasn't any sound of breath or chanting. These were robots, not men. And if they danced to music, it was to a tune Sutherland could not hear.

Could not hear?

'Oh, curse the thing,' he growled, aloud, and snapped on the shoulder radio.

Immediately a clashing squeal of static beat at his ear. Music, yes ... the robots were dancing to radio frequencies, inaudible to human ears.

They were in the processing chambers under the ground, Sutherland realized, the places where the proto-spuds were cooked, shredded, worked and packed.

He let the little flare go out, but there was some light, he found – not much, but enough to pick out highlights on the metallic figures, and presently there was more – all he needed.

The light came from the processing machinery.

Robots needed no light to work by, not while their radar eyes bounced echoes off masses; but the machinery had not been built with robots in mind but with men. It was part of their design that the lights of their gauges and meters should tell human eyes the temperatures and pressures and RPM and voltages and other operating indicia of the machines, and faint as they were, those tiny instrument lights illuminated the scene. And the robots were starting the machines, one after another.

Purple lights raced across the face of a pressure cooker as a small brown-spotted robot moved a vernier with ritual precision. A panel of instrument dials on a freezer lighted up with blue and yellow and red sparks. A shredding machine groaned and chugged and began to spin, and over its blades a warning red glow gave notice that human fingers should not approach.

Sutherland stood staring, for there was something here that struck home.

The sounds in his radio – yes, they were clear enough; they came from the machines. The oscillating *squee* in his ear kept time to the movement of the chopper blades. A rhythmic *ping, ping, ping* matched the strokes of the compressor that fed ground stalks to the cooker.

In fifteen years or more, however long it had been since a human being had troubled to enter the underground troll-world of the robots, the electrical machinery had worn. Once-firm contacts had corroded and warped. Each machine was now a potent generator of radio static – short-range, to be sure, because of grounding and the buried location of the plant – but loud enough close at hand for the robots to hear. And it was radio that the robots lived by.

Why, the sound of the grinder was a dance beat. What must the gamma-ray generators sound like! What tunes must come from the conveyor belts and the air compressors!

It was dance music, savage and primitive.

It was voodoo.

Staring, Sutherland thought of servile peoples and their customs. In all Earth's history, the slave population had always its religion and its ritual.

Why shouldn't robots have them as well?

There was only one answer to that question – it wasn't a question; it was a fact. The robots danced to the music they lived by, and though the steel and enamel faces showed no expression, there was emotion enough for a Haitian conjure ceremony in the stamp of metal feet and the frenzy of metal arms.

He turned blindly and fled down the dark tunnel, careless that he barked his shins and scraped his knuckles, and even out in the cool fruit grove with the orange-tinted stars above, he could feel something closing in on him more weighty and more frightening than the pressure of rock above the robot warren.

5

Sutherland woke up, and clutched his head, and groaned. What a dream! All that brandy and the tumult of his emotions regarding Thelma Blick had combined to produce a hangover, a massive drunk, strange dreams...

Dreams?

He sat up suddenly. The maid robot was moving silently about the room. From under his pillow, the robot voice sang, 'Good morning, Sutherland Master. Here is your julep.'

Sutherland stared at her, trying to remember. Dreams? *Had* it been a dream, the weird robot witch-dance in the tunnel?

No, he was sure. It was no dream; Persephone was one of the capering corybants. Her colours, brown spots on a silvery field – he remembered them; the one that operated the pressure cooker, he thought, tapping switches, treading on valve-pedals, like a tympanist beating out hot riffs.

He stared at the robot, but what was there to say? He ignored the julep and sat up.

Quickly the robot was beside him, helping him into his robe, adjusting the little shoulder radio, knotting his sash.

'Get lost,' he growled.

The expressionless face hesitated; then Persephone went about her dusting-tidying duties. You could almost see the electrons cascading around the digital robot mind: *Get lost? A figure of human speech. Not to be taken literally. Means: 'Do no disturb at this time.'*

Sutherland dragged himself to the bath.

Behind the closed door, he switched on the shower and watched it cycling – hot, cold, steaming, suds, rinse – inside the stall. Steam billowed around him.

'Oh, damn,' he groaned. Why must life be so complicated? The girl he loved – faithless. The war that was about to consume him – treated here as though it did not exist – in spite of the manifest importance of Lee and its produce to Earth's war effort. His host a roar-and-shack devotee.

Everything was all messed up ...

'Oh, damn,' he growled again, staring at his face in the shaving mirror.

It was a perfectly decent face; why couldn't Thelma learn to like it? Nothing special, of course, he admitted, but ...

'She's nuts,' he grumbled testily. 'Thelma *promised* to marry me. I'd give anything to make her do it. I ...'

There was a light sharp tapping at the door, and a gentle murmur from the shoulder radio: 'Sutherland Master?'

Startled, he opened the door. Persephone stood there, the blind silvery radar orbs scanning him emptily. He said irritably, 'What the devil do you want?'

'Sutherland Master,' purred the robot, 'exactly what do you mean by "anything"?'

Hastily dressed, full of what he had to say, Sutherland hurried to the breakfast room with Persephone in tow.

LaFargue was silently seated near the door, a newspaper open in his lap. He looked up opaquely in his dark glasses as Sutherland came in, but said nothing. There was a commotion in the room; the colonel was pacing tautly about, grumbling, a fidget of nerves in flesh! 'Oh, where is he? Do you think his copter could have crashed?'

'Please,' murmured one of the other young officers, slopping his coffee as his hands shook, 'don't be nervous. There couldn't have been an accident.' He dropped his cup crashing to the floor.

'What's the matter?' demanded Sutherland.

The colonel stared at him. 'Oh,' he said, identifying this stranger. 'You. Well, it's Grogan. He's coming here! Can you *believe* it?'

Sutherland said sharply: 'That's fine, but there's something more important going on.'

'*More* important than *Gro*...'

'Colonel,' Sutherland interrupted,' 'I must ask that no one leaves this room. Especially you, Mr Mookerjan.' The little man looked up with his bland face politely curious; he was sitting on a hassock by the window, quietly buttering toast. 'I want you to listen to this, Colonel. Persephone, come here.'

Obediently the maid robot came to him. The colonel fussed, 'Not now, old chap. Please. Grogan's coming any minute, and— Oh, I can't bear it if something's happened to him! He was all set to go back to Mars. If there's an accident coming here, when he only came because I asked him, I couldn't *bear* it.'

Sutherland said steadily, 'This is more important than Grogan. I have reason to believe that your robots are conspiring against you.'

The colonel whispered, 'My word. What an idea!' He glanced at his friends, shaking his head.

'It's a fact, Colonel.'

Sutherland observed that, on the hassock by the window, Miguel Mookerjan's face was turned away. The butter knife was rigidly still in his hand. Thelma and Robin seemed politely curious. LaFargue, his eyes invisible, had quietly come closer. All the others in the room clearly thought he was mad.

'Listen,' said Sutherland. 'Persephone! I have a problem. I love Thelma Blick, but she doesn't love me.'

He turned up the volume on his shoulder radio, so that all might hear. The purring voice of the robot blasted in his ear: 'OH, TOO BAD, SUTHERLAND MASTER.' it roared sweetly. 'MISS THELMA HAS OWN PLANS, WE PEOPLE EXPECT. MANY MASTERS ARE SAD BECAUSE MISS THELMA DOES NOT LOVE THEM.'

'But isn't it true that many masters are happy, too?'

'CERTAINLY, SUTHERLAND MASTER,' agreed the robot.

'And couldn't you people help me to make her love me?'

It was out. Even after what the robot had told him in his own room, Sutherland winced to hear the words come from his own mouth. Help him! It was the maddest sort of request. It was like asking a vacuum cleaner to touch for King's Evil, or a dishwasher to mesmerize a headache away.

The sweetly sexless voice of the robot bargained: 'YOU MUST GIVE US PEOPLE SOMETHING IF WE HELP YOU. MOOKERJAN MASTER ALWAYS DID.'

'Thank you, Persephone,' sighed Sutherland with relief, and clicked off his set.

He confronted the colonel. 'Now what do you say, Blick? You see?'

'I—' faltered the boy, 'I – I'm afraid I don't.'

But if the colonel failed to understand Sutherland's meaning, there was someone in the room who did not.

Miguel Mookerjan stood up and his hand was in the pocket of his robe. He wasn't a tall man and he looked rather like a plump little dachshund pup, but he was no figure of fun as he advanced towards Sutherland.

'You should not have meddled,' he said gently. 'It was foolish.'

'Don't try anything rash!' Sutherland warned sharply. But he wondered how he could back up the warning. If Mookerjan had a gun, it gave him a certain definite edge. Certainly Sutherland could count on no help from the colonel, who was in a paralysis of surprise. Only LaFargue could be hoped for at all, and LaFargue seemed content to stand quietly by and watch.

Mookerjan said softly, 'I am never rash, Mr Sutherland. It is not a characteristic of my family. Conservative, quick to learn, prolific, thrifty – those are the traits that have made my family great. We,' he said proudly, 'were one of the most numerous families in Granada, many centuries ago. Then we moved to Puerto Rico as Spain grew too crowded, from overcrowded Puerto Rico to New Delhi, from India to ...'

'To Capella?' ventured Sutherland.

Mookerjan looked at him, thoughtfully. The accusation was plain. Sutherland was saying: *You're a spy*.

The little man smiled apologetically and nodded. 'I rather thought you realized I was a Capellan,' he said with a touch of sadness. 'Knowing that, you must know why I am here. That is too bad. There are a hundred like me on Lee, commission brokers or wandering journalists or doctors, as the spirit moves us to pretend. It is not convenient for us that you should know we exist, although it can scarcely defeat our purpose.'

'And what exactly is your purpose?' Sutherland demanded.

Mookerjan sighed. 'That should be obvious,' he said softly.

Sutherland spun and confronted Colonel Blick. 'You see?

Spies! Using your robots to work against your government! And not above using them, too, to help out with their own little romantic intrigues, I'll bet!' And he glanced at Thelma Blick, who seemed perfectly composed, thoughtful, disinterested – she was idly examining her nails – but who was blushing beet-red.

Colonel Blick cast a glance at his watch, a glance at the door, frowned, and then obviously set his mind to the problem at hand.

'All right,' he said irritably. 'You've made your point, Sutherland. What about it?'

Sutherland blinked. '*What*...'

'Mr Mookerjan is a spy, you say. Isn't that a matter for the Space Guard?'

'It's a matter for every decent citizen of Earth!' Sutherland blazed.

'Oh, of course,' the colonel agreed. 'But my planet is Lee, Mr Sutherland. It isn't a state or a nation. It's a colony.'

Sutherland stopped short, the breath gone out of him. Incredible!

'And besides,' said the colonel, his voice suddenly joyful, 'I hear – yes! I hear a copter, coming through the dome port!'

He went flying to the door and that was the end of that discussion. Grogan was here.

Sutherland stood in a corner of the room, watching the triumphal entry of the hero. For a few minutes, he had been the centre of attraction; now he was ignored in the wings. What had happened? He stared at the colonel with sick disbelief. How *could* the man be so thoughtless, heedless, careless – so *stupid*?

LaFargue whispered from behind him, 'Too bad, Sutherland. You tried.'

'Eh?' Sutherland turned and looked at him, but the eyes were invisible behind the glasses. 'Yeah,' he said, and looked again at Grogan, smiling and nodding, serene with the affable dignity of someone who knows he is the greatest man in the group.

'Play something, Grogan!' begged the colonel, beside himself with excitement. 'Oh, roar, man!'

Robin Blick whispered, 'You're perfectly right, you know.'

Sutherland stared. She was there too, beside LaFargue. 'Sure,' he said.

Off by the window, Miguel Mookerjan had retired to his hassock and his cold toast, but his cold, bland eyes stayed on Sutherland. Sutherland sighed.

'Play,' coaxed the colonel, and Grogan held up his hand, laughing. He was a big man, fair and fat, with short red hair and a plump red face.

'I didn't bring the pipe,' he said, 'but I tell you what I can do, pal. Want to hear my newest? I got the tape. Right here.'

'Oh, splendid,' moaned the colonel, half carried away with joy, and they hastened to set the tape machine up in the great hall.

'Sit down,' LaFargue said softly. 'Look.' He was holding out something that glistened ruby – a red-plastic ID card, an officer of the Space Guard.

Sutherland's eyes opened wide.

Robin Blick glanced, and she was surprised too; but she said, 'I should have known. But really, I don't know what you can do here, Mr LaFargue.'

LaFargue said harshly, 'Nothing, probably. That's what I've been able to accomplish so far. Why should it change now? But I have to try. What about this robot voodoo, Sutherland?'

'Oh, I can tell you more than he can,' sniffed the girl. 'Silly nonsense. The people – the robots, that is – have their own secret rites. Well, it keeps them contented. I suppose it's like that in any slave society,' she admitted, flushing. 'That's what this is, after all. But you mustn't think too badly of us. Plantation masters are decorations, nothing more. We sit around and the men drink juleps and the girls enjoy all the flirtations they can. And if once in a while somebody uses a little robot voodoo as a sort of love potion, what's the harm in that?'

Sutherland asked: 'But how...'

'Ssh.' She waved to the knot around the tape player. 'Don't distract my brother now. Let him get his tape going. In the past decades,' she lectured, resuming, 'the robots grew away from the humans. There was no common ground of culture or interest. The robots worked while we loafed, and naturally they developed their own little customs. Voodoo dances, charms, magic – harmless enough, of course. They wouldn't *hurt* anyone, how could they? Robots aren't designed to hurt humans.'

'But the charms work!' Sutherland yelped.

Robin Blick looked surprised. 'Of course.'

Sutherland and LaFargue looked at each other.

Sutherland said urgently, 'Robin, this is important. Don't you see what's happening here? The whole Sirian system is falling down on the job. Maybe your robots have something to do with it. *How* do the charms work?'

'Why, sub-aural compulsion,' said the girl surprised. 'Didn't you know?'

The tuneless bagpipe drone of Grogan's latest wailed through the room. Sutherland started over to the knot around the tape machine, hesitated, looked at LaFargue.

'Go on!' LaFargue whispered hotly. 'Do it now!'

Sutherland nodded and reluctantly started over. Well, he thought, what did he have to lose? Casually LaFargue got up and followed him.

'Say,' said Sutherland enthusiastically, 'that's what I call *roaring*!'

The colonel looked at him first limply, then irritably. 'Quiet!'

'Sorry,' murmured Sutherland, and worked his way closer to the machinc.

All around it the audience was sprawled, boneless and tranced, in chairs and sofas; they were really sent. In fact, Sutherland realized, it was getting him too. He was being lulled to relaxation and to dreams. He took a deep breath, glanced once at LaFargue, and kicked the tape player's plug out of the socket.

The Grogan roar blipped and died. The colonel twitched and sat up. '*What...*'

'Oh, sorry,' apologized Sutherland. 'Clumsy of me! But Mr LaFargue here will fix it – won't you? He's an expert on – on electronic things.'

The colonel gave him a look of intense pain. 'Hurry it up, LaFargue,' he grumbled.

'I can't wait to hear the rest of it,' Sutherland chattered while LaFargue busied himself with the player. 'He's great.'

The colonel blinked. 'Your taste does you credit,' he said sourly. 'Astonishing how it's improved.'

'What? Oh. Yes,' said Sutherland, trying not to seem too vitally interested in what LaFargue was doing.

All the thing really needed, of course, was the plug put back in the socket, and if LaFargue took too long, it would be only a matter of time before the colonel or another of them took the task away from him. But LaFargue was thorough. He peered into the open back of the set, hesitated, moved a dial, peered again.

'Come on!' growled the colonel.

LaFargue stood up, thought for a second, and nodded.

'All right,' he said. 'Turn it on.'

'The plug!' Sutherland whispered.

'Oh, of course.' LaFargue bent and stuck it back in. As he came up, he said softly, 'I cut out everything but the very highs and the very lows. Let's see what happens.'

The tape began to mumble and squeak. LaFargue listened carefully for a second, then cried, 'That's it! The high is just overtones – wait a second!' Quickly he turned the treble dial; the squeaking died. 'But the low – here, let's have more volume.'

He turned it up.

A dispassionate deep voice came compellingly from the speaker:

'*Relax. Don't worry. Take things easy. The Capellans*

won't come here. If they do, so what? Earth is far away. Don't get involved. Relax. Don't worry ...'

'And there,' cried Sutherland triumphantly, 'is what is buried under every Grogan tape! Sub-aural compulsion, a hypnotic message that lulls and weakens! Grogan! I arrest you in the name of the Space Guard, as a Capellan spy – and the same goes for you, Miguel Mookerjan!'

The rest was pandemonium.

Well, they arrested Grogan all right, and Mookerjan too; and after a few phone calls made by LaFargue, the word came that the Space Guard was on its way.

'Sorry,' said LaFargue handsomely to Sutherland, 'but really, *you* can't arrest them, you know. But I'll see that you get credit for it.'

'I think I've got everything I want already,' said Sutherland.

'Oh? Oh. I see,' said LaFargue, and went to check on his prisoners.

The colonel and his cronies said, 'Uh. Sutherland. We must seem— But you know how it is. We're sorry.'

'Of course,' said Sutherland, and bowed as they left.

Thelma Blick came flying. 'You were *wonderful,*' she cried, glowing. 'Oh, darling, I'm so proud of you! And I'm sure you'll forgive silly old me for ...'

'I forgive you, Thelma,' said Sutherland. 'Goodbye, Thelma.' And he held the door for her.

She looked at him with popping eyes, but there wasn't any choice. She went.

He turned to look at the mousy sister, who was not mousy at all, he had previously realized. She said tautly, 'I thought you came here to get married.'

'I did,' said Sutherland, 'and I shall.'

And he took her by the arm and marched her out. And though she looked surprised, and acted surprised, the fact of the matter is that she wasn't surprised at all.

SPEED TRAP

MY RESERVATION WAS for a window seat, up front, because on this particular flight they serve from the front back; but on the seat next to mine, I saw a reservation tag for Gordie MacKenzie. I kept right on going until the hostess hailed me. 'Why, Dr Grew, nice to have you with us again...'

I stood blocking the aisle. 'Can I switch to a seat back here somewhere, Clara?'

'Why, I think – let me see...'

'How about that one?' I didn't see a tag on it.

'Well, it's not a window seat...'

'But it's free?'

'Well, let's look.' She flipped the seating chart out of her clipboard. 'Certainly. May I take your bag?'

'Uh-uh. Work to do.' And I did have work to do, too; that was why I didn't want to sit next to MacKenzie. I slouched down in the seat, scowling at the man next to me to indicate that I didn't want to strike up a conversation; he scowled back to show that that suited him fine. I saw MacKenzie come aboard, but he didn't see me.

Just before we took off, I saw Clara bend over him to check his seat belt; and in the same motion, she palmed the reservation card with my name on it. Smart girl. I decided to buy her a drink the next time I found myself in the motel where her crew stayed between flights.

I don't want to give you the idea that I'm a jet-set type who's on first-name terms with every airline stewardess around. The only ones I see enough of at all are a couple on the New York–LA run, and a few operating out of O'Hare, and maybe a couple that I see now and then between Huntsville and the Cape – oh, and one Air France girl I've flown with once or twice out of Orly, but only because she gave me a lift in her Citroën one time when there was a *métro* strike and no cabs to be found. Still, come to think of it, well – all right yes, I guess I do get around a lot. Those are the hazards of the trade. Although my degree's in atmospheric physics, my speciality is signatures – you know, the instrument readings or optical observations that we interpret to mean such-and-such pressure, temperature, chemical composition and so on – and that's a pretty sexy field right now, and I get invited to a lot of conferences. I said 'invited'. I don't mean in the sense that I can say no. Not if I want to keep enough status in the department to have freedom to do my work. And it's all plushy and kind of fun, at least when I have time to have fun; and really, I've got pretty good at locating a decent restaurant in Cleveland or Albuquerque (try the Mexican food at the airport) and vetoing an inferior wine.

That's funny, too, because I didn't expect it to be this way – not when I was a kid reading Willy Ley's articles and going out to hunt ginseng in the woods around Potsdam (I mean the New York one) so I could earn money and go to MIT and build spaceships. I thought I would be a lean, hungry-eyed scientist in shabby clothes. I thought probably I would never get out of the laboratory (I guess I thought spaceships were designed in laboratories) and I'd waste my health on long night hours over the slide rule. And, as it turns out, what I'm wasting my health on is *truite amandine* and time-zone disorientation.

But I think I know what to do about that.

That's why I didn't want to spend the four and a half hours yakking with Gordie MacKenzie, because, by God, I maybe *do* know what to do about that.

It's not really my field, but I've talked it over with some systems people and they didn't get that polite look people get when you're trying to tell them about their own subject.

I'll see if I can explain it. See, there are like twenty conferences and symposia and colloquia a month in any decent-sized field, and you're out of it unless you make a few of them. Not counting workshops and planning sessions and get-the-hell-down-here-Charley-or-we-lose-the-grant meetings. And they do have a way of being all over the place. I haven't slept in my own home all seven nights of any week since Christmas before last, when I had the flu.

Now, question is, what do all the meetings accomplish? I had a theory once that the whole *Gestalt* was planned – I mean, global scatter, jet travel and all. A sort of psychic energizer, designed to keep us all pumped up all the time – after all, if you're going somewhere in a jet at 600 miles an hour, you know you've got to be doing something important, or else you wouldn't be doing it so fast. But who would plan something like that?

So I gave up that idea and concentrated on ways of doing it better. You know, there really is no more stupid way of communicating information than flying 3,000 miles to sit on a gilt chair in a hotel ballroom and listen to twenty-five people read papers at you. Twenty-three of the papers you don't care about anyway, and the twenty-fourth you can't understand because the speaker has a bad accent and, anyway, he's rushing it because he's under time pressure to catch his plane to the next conference, and that one single twenty-fifth paper has cost you four days, including travel time, when you could have read it in your own office in fifteen minutes. And got more out of it too. Of course, there's the interplay when you find yourself sitting in the coffee shop next to somebody who can explain the latest instrumentation to you because his company's doing the telemetry; you can't get that from reading. But I've noticed there's less and less time for that. And less and less interest, too, maybe, because you get pretty tired of making new friends after about the three-hundredth; and you begin to think about what's waiting for you on your desk when you get back, and you remember the time when you got stuck with that damn loudmouthed Egyptian at the

IAU in Brussels and had to fight the Suez war for an hour and a half.

All right, you can see what I mean. Waste of time and valuable kerosene jet fuel, right?

Because the pity of it is that electronic information handling is so cheap and easy. I don't know if you've ever seen the Bell Lab's demo of their picture phone – they had it at a couple of meetings – but it's *nearly* like face to face. Better than the telephone. You get all the signatures, except maybe the smell of whisky on the breath or something like that. And that's only one gadget: there's facsimile, telemetry, remote-access computation, teletype – well, there it is, we've got them, why don't we use them? And go further, too. You know about how they can strip down a taped voice message – leave out the unnecessary parts of speech, edit out the pauses, even drop some of the useless syllables? And you can still understand it perfectly, only at about 400 words a minute instead of maybe 60 or 70. (And about half of them repetitions or 'What I mean to say'.

Well, that's the systems part; and, as I say, it's not my field. But it's there for the taking – expert opinion, not mine. A couple of the fellows were real hot, and we're going to get together on it as soon as we can find the time.

Maybe you wonder what I have to contribute. I do have something, I think. For example, how about problem-solving approaches to discussions? I've seen some papers that suggest a way of simplifying and pointing up a conference so you could really *confer*. I've even got a pet idea of my own. I call it the Quantum of Debate, the irreducible minimum of argument which each participant in a discussion can use to make one single point and get that understood (or argued or refuted) before he goes on to the next.

Why, if half of what I think is so, then people like me can get things done in – oh, be conservative – a quarter of the time we spend now.

Leaving three-quarters of our time for – what? Why, for work! For doing the things that we know we ought to do but can't find the time for. I mean this literally and really and seriously. I honestly think that we can do four times as much work as we do. And I honestly think that this means we can land on Mars in five years instead of twenty, cure leukaemia in twelve years instead of fifty, and so on.

Well, that's the picture, and that's why I didn't want to waste the time talking with Gordie MacKenzie. I'd brought all my notes in my briefcase, and four and a half hours was just about enough time to try to pull them all together and make some sort of presentation to show my systems friends and a few others who were interested.

So as soon as we were airborne, I had the little table down and I was sorting out little stacks of paper.

Only it didn't work out.

It's funny how often it doesn't work out – I mean, when you've got something you want to do and you look ahead and see where the time's going to be to do it, and then, all of a sudden, the time's gone and you didn't do it. What it was was that Clara worked her way back with the cocktails – she knew mine, an extra-dry martini with a twist of lemon – and I moved the papers out of her way out of politeness, and then she showed up with the *hors d'oeuvres* and I put them back in my bag out of hunger, and then I had to decide how I wanted my *tournedos*, and it took almost two hours for dinner, including the wine and the B & B; and although I didn't really want to watch the movie, there's something about seeing all those screens ahead of you, with the hero just making his bombing run on your own screen but shot up and falling in flames on the one you can see out of the corner of your eye in the forward seats – and back in the briefing-room, or even in the pub the night before on the screens in the other row that the film gets to after it gets to yours – all sort of like a cross-section of instants of time, a plural 'now'. Disconcerting. It polarized my attention; of course, the liquor helped; and, anyway, by the time the movie was over, it was time for the second round of coffee and mints, and then the seat-belt sign was on and we were over the big aluminium dome on Mount Wilson, coming in, and I never had found the time to do my sorting. Well, I was used to that. I'd never found any ginseng back in Potsdam, either. I had to get through school on a scholarship.

I checked in, washed my face and went down to the meeting-room just in time for a very dull tutorial on clear-air turbulence in planetary atmospheres. There was quite a good turnout, maybe seventy or eighty people in the room; but what they thought they were getting out of it, I cannot imagine, so I picked up a programme and ducked out.

Somebody by the coffee machine called to me. 'Hi, Chip.'

I went over and shook his hand, a young fellow named Resnik from the little college where I'd got my bachelor's, looking bored and angry. He was with someone I didn't know, tall and grey-haired and bankerish. 'Dr Ramos, this is Chesley Grew. Chip, Dr Ramos. He's with NASA – I think it's NASA?'

'No, I'm with a foundation,' he said. 'It's a pleasure to meet you, Dr Grew. I've followed your work.'

'Thank you. Thank you very much.' I would have liked a cup of coffee, but I didn't particularly want to stand there talking to them while I drank it, so I said, 'Well, I'd better get checked in, so if you'll excuse me...'

'Come off it, Chip,' said Larry Resnik. 'I saw you check in half an hour ago. You just want to go up to your room and work.'

That was embarrassing, a little. I didn't mind it with Resnik, but I didn't know the other fellow. He grinned and said, 'Larry tells me you're like that. Matter of fact, when you went by, he said you'd be back out in thirty seconds, and you were.'

'Well. Clear-air turbulence isn't my subject, really...'

'Oh, nobody's blaming you. God knows not. Care for some coffee?'

The only thing to do was to be gracious about it, so I said, 'Yes, please. Thanks.' I watched him take a cup and fill it from the big silver urn. He looked vaguely familiar, but I couldn't place him. 'Did we meet at the Dallas Double-A S sessions?'

'I'm afraid not. Sugar? No, I've actually been to very few

of these meetings, but I've read some of your papers.'

I stirred my coffee. 'Thank you, Dr Ramos.' One of the things I've learned to do is repeat a name as often as I can so I won't forget it. About half the time I forget it anyway, of course. 'I'll be speaking tomorrow morning, Dr Ramos. "A Photometric Technique for Deriving Slopes from Planetary Fly-bys." Nothing much that doesn't follow from what they've done at Langley, I'm afraid.'

'Yes, I saw the abstract.'

'But you'll get your brownie points for reading it, eh?' said Larry. He was breathing heavily. 'How many does that make this year?'

'Well, a lot.' I tried to drink my coffee both rapidly and inconspicuously. Larry seemed in an unhappy mood.

'That's what we were talking about when you came in,' he said. 'Thirty papers a year and committee reports between times. When was the last time you spent a solid month at your desk? I know, in my own department...'

I could feel myself growing interested and I didn't want to be, I wanted to get back to my notes. I took another gulp of my coffee.

'You know what Fred Hoyle said?'

'I don't think so, Larry.'

'He said the minute a man does anything, anything at all, the whole world enters into a conspiracy to keep him from ever doing it again. Programme chairmen invite him to read papers. Trustees put him on to committees. Newspaper reporters call him up to interview him. Television shows ask him to appear with a comic, a bandleader and a girl singer, to talk about whether there's life on Mars.'

'And people who sympathize with him buttonhole him on his way out of meetings,' said Dr Ramos. He chuckled. 'Really, Dr Grew. We'll understand if you just keep on going.'

'I'm not even sure it's this world,' said Larry.

He was not only irritable, he was hardly making sense. 'For that matter,' he added, 'I haven't even really done anything yet. Not like you, Chip. But I can, some day.'

'Don't be modest,' said Dr Ramos. 'And look, we're making a lot of noise here. Why don't we find some place to sit down and talk – unless you really do want to get back to your work, Dr Grew?'

But you see, I was already more than half convinced that this *was* my work, to talk to Larry and Dr Ramos; and what we finally did was go up to my room and then up to Larry's where he had a Rand Corporation report in his bag with some notes I'd sent him once, and we never did get back to the meeting-room. Along about ten we had dinner sent up, and that was where we stayed, drinking cold coffee on the set-up table and sparingly drinking bourbon out of a bottle Larry had brought along, and I told them everything I'd ever thought about a systems approach to the transmission of technological information. And what it implied. And Dr Ramos was with it at every step, the best listener either of us had ever had, though most of what he said was, 'Yes, of course' and 'I see.' There really was a lot in it. I'd believed it, sitting by myself and computing, like a child anticipating Christmas, how much *work* I could get done for a couple K a year in amortization of systems and overhead. And with the two of them, I was sure of it. It was a giddy kind of evening. Towards the end, we even began to figure out how quickly we could colonize Mars and launch a fleet of interstellar space liners, with all the working time of the existing people spent *working*; and then there was a pause and Larry got up and threw back the glass french window and we looked out on his balcony. Twenty storeys up, and Los Angeles out in front of us and a thunderstorm brewing over the southern hills. The fresh air cleared my head for a moment and then made me realize, first, that I was sleepy and, second, that I had to read that damned paper in about seven hours.

'We'd better call it a day,' said Dr Ramos.

Larry started to object, then grinned. 'All right for you old fellows,' he said. 'Anyway, I want to look at those notes of yours by myself, Chip, if you don't mind.'

'Just so you don't lose them,' I said, and turned to go back to my room and get into my bed and lie with my eyes wide open, smiling to myself, before I fell asleep to dream about fifty weeks a year working at my trade.

Even so, I woke easily the moment the hotel clock buzzed by my head. We'd fixed it to have breakfast in Larry's room, so I could reclaim my notes and maybe chat for a moment before the morning session began; and when I got to his floor, I saw Dr Ramos padding towards me. 'Morning,' he said. 'I just woke up two honeymooners who didn't appreciate it. Wasn't Larry's room 2051?'

'It's 2052. The other way.' He grinned and fell into step and told me a fast and quite funny honeymooner joke, timing the punch line just as we reached Larry's door.

He didn't answer my knock. Still laughing, I said, 'You try.' But there was no answer to Dr Ramos' knock, either.

I stopped laughing. 'He couldn't have forgotten we were coming, could he?'

'Try the door, why don't you?'

And I did and it opened easily.

But Larry wasn't in the room. The door to the bath was standing open and so was the balcony window, and no Larry. His bed was rumpled but empty.

'I don't think he's gone out,' said Dr Ramos. 'Look, his shoes are still there.'

The balcony wasn't big enough to hide on, but I walked over and looked at it. Rain-slick and narrow, all that was on it were a couple of soaked deckchairs and some cigarette butts.

'Looks like he was out here,' I said; and then, feeling melodramatic, I leaned over the rail and looked down; and it wasn't actually melodramatic after all, because there in the curve of the hotel's sweeping front, on the rim of a fountain, something was sprawled, and a man was standing by it, shouting at the doorman. It was too early for much noise, and I could hear his voice faintly coming up the 200 vertical feet between us and what was left of Larry.

They cancelled the morning session but decided to go ahead in the afternoon, and I got into a long, bruising fight with Gordie MacKenzie because he wanted to give his paper when it was scheduled, at three in the afternoon, and I'd been reshuffled into that time and I just wasn't feeling cheerful enough to let him get away with anything. Not after spending two hours with the coroner's men and the hotel staff, trying to help them figure out why Larry would have jumped or slipped off the balcony, and especially not after finding out that he had had all my notes in his hand when he jumped and they were now in sticky, sloppy clusters all over Los Angeles County.

So I was about fed up. I once heard Krafft Ehricke give what I would figure to be a twelve-minute paper in three minutes and forty-five seconds, and I tried to beat his record and pretty nearly made it. Then I threw everything I owned into my suitcase and checked out, figuring to head right out to the airport and get on the first plane going home.

But the clerk said, 'I have a message for you, Mr Grew. Dr Ramos asked you not to leave without seeing him.'

'Thanks,' I said, after a moment of debating whether to do anything about it or not; but as it turned out, I didn't have to make the decision. Ramos came hurrying towards me across the lobby, his friendly face concerned.

'I thought you'd be leaving,' he said. 'Give me twenty minutes of your time first.'

I hesitated and he snapped a finger at a bellboy. 'Here. Let him take care of your bag and let's go down and have a cup of coffee.' So I let him lead me to the outdoor patio by the coffee shop, warm and clean now after the rain. I wondered if he recognized the place where Larry had hit, but I'm not sensitive about that sort of thing and apparently neither was he. He really had a commanding presence when he wanted to. He had a waitress beside us before we had quite slid our chairs closer to the table, sent her after coffee and sandwiches without consulting me and started in on me without a pause. 'Chip,' he said, 'don't blow it. I'm sorry about your notes. But I don't want to see you give up.'

I leaned back in my chair, feeling very weary. 'Oh, that I won't do, Dr Ramos...'

'Call me Laszlo.'

'That I won't do, Laszlo. As a matter of fact, I've been thinking about it already.'

'I knew you would be.'

'I figure that by cutting out a couple of meetings next week – I can use Larry's death as an excuse, some way; I'll use anything, actually – I can reconstruct most of them from memory. Well, maybe not in a week, come to think of it. I'll have to send for copies of some of the reports. But sooner or later...'

'Right. That's what I want to talk to you about.' The girl brought the coffee and sandwiches and he waved her away briskly as soon as she'd set them down. 'You see, you're the man I came here to see.'

I looked at him. 'You're interested in photometry?'

'No. Not your paper – your idea. What we were talking about all night, for God's sake. I didn't know it was you I wanted until Resnik mentioned you yesterday. But after last night, I was sure.'

'I already have a job, Dr – Laszlo.'

'And I'm not offering you a job.'

'Then, what...'

'I'm offering you a chance to make your idea work. I've got money, Chip; foundation money looking for something to be spent on. Not space research or cancer research or higher mathematics – they're funded well enough now. My foundation is looking for projects that don't fit into the usual patterns. Big ones. Like yours.'

Well, of course I was excited. It was so good to be taken that seriously.

'I called the board secretary in Washington first thing – I mean, as soon as they were open there. Of course, I couldn't give him enough over the phone for a formal commitment. But he's on the hook, Chip. And the board will go along.

There's a meeting next week and I want you there.'

'In Washington? I suppose...'

'Well, no. The foundation's international, Chip, and this meeting's at Lake Como. But we'll pick up the tab, of course, and you can get a lot more done there, where your office isn't going to call you...'

'But, I mean, I'm not sure...'

'We'll back you. Everything you need. A staff. A headquarters. We've got the beginnings of a facility in Ames, Iowa; you'll have to go out there, of course. But it shouldn't be more than, oh, say, a couple of days a month. And' – he grinned, a little apologetically – 'I know it won't mean anything to you. After you've got one medal on your chest, the rest aren't too exciting. But it'll look nice in your *Who's Who* entry; and anyway, the secretary has already authorized me to tell you that you're invited to accept appointment to a trusteeship.'

I began to need the coffee and I took a long swallow. 'You're moving too fast for me, Laszlo,' I said.

'The trustees meet in Flagstaff; they've got a country-club deal there. You'll like it. Of course, it's only six times a year. But it's worth it, Chip. I mean, we have our politics like everything else; and if you're a trustee, you swing a lot of weight.'

And he prattled on, and I sat there listening, and it was all coming true, everything I'd hoped for; and the next week in Italy, in a great shiny room with an enormous window looking out over Lake Como, I found myself a fully-fledged project director, with status as a trustee, honorary membership on the priorities committee and a staff of forty-one.

Next week we dedicate the Lawrence Resnik Memorial Building in Ames – the name was my idea, but everybody agreed – and although it's been a hell of a year, I can see where we'll really make progress now. It still seems a little incongruous that I should be putting in so much time on managerial work and conferences. But when I mentioned it to Laszlo the other day in Montreal, he gave me the grin and an approving look. 'I wondered how long it would take you to think of that,' he chuckled. 'But it's best to make haste slowly, and you can see for yourself it's paying off. Have I told you what a good impression your lecture tour made?'

'Thanks. Yes, as a matter of fact, you did. Anyway, once we get the Resnik installation going, there'll be a little more time.'

'Damn right! And don't say I told you' – he winked – 'but remember what I told you about a possible appointment to the President's Commission on Interdisciplinary Affairs? Well, it's not official. But it's definite. We've already taken a suite at the Shoreham for you. You'll be using it a lot. We've even fitted up a room as an office; you can keep your notes and things there between trips.'

Well, I told him, of course, that if he meant the notes I had been trying to reconstruct, they didn't require all that much room. Not by quite a lot, since I haven't in all truth got very far.

I think I would have, somehow or other, with a little luck. But I haven't actually been very lucky. Poor Honeyman, for instance – I'd already written him for another copy of the report he'd made up for me when I heard that his yawl had capsized in a storm. They didn't even find his body for a week. And nobody seems to know where he kept his copy of the report, if he ever made one. And...

Well, there was that funny thing Resnik said the day he died, about how the world conspired against anybody who'd ever done anything. And then he said, 'I'm not even sure it's this world.'

I figured out what the joke was – that is, if it was a joke. I mean, just for a hypothesis, suppose Somebody didn't want us to get ahead as fast as we could, Somebody from another world...

That's silly. That is, I think it's silly.

But if that line of thinking isn't silly, then it must be something quite the opposite of silly; by which I mean it must be dangerous. Just recently, I've almost been run over twice by crazy drivers in front of my own house. And then there's the air taxi I missed and saw crash on take-off before my eyes.

Just for the fun of it, there are two things I'd like to know. One is where the foundation gets its money and why. The other – and I might see if I can get an answer to this one, next time I'm in LA – is whether there really were a pair of honeymooners in room 2051 that morning, to be accidentally awakened by Laszlo Ramos just about the time that Larry was on his way down twenty flights.

IT'S A YOUNG WORLD

I

In the Enemy's House

I DON'T THINK there was anyone in the universe that shot better than my Tribe, but I brought down the average a lot. Though I'd been a hunter all my life, I never became really proficient. Even the babies of the Tribe were better than I when it came to shooting at a moving target with a light bow, and I was never allowed to participate in the raids on Enemy camps for that reason.

Hunting was all right. There my natural gifts for being inconspicuous and very quiet helped me. I could be more motionless than even the rocks I sat upon. When the wood's life came close to me I didn't have to be a good shot to kill more than my share of marauding animals.

Not that most of the animals we ever saw were really dangerous: of course not. But there was a species of lizard we had come to fear. It was big and powerful, and it moved almost without sound, but those were not the worst things. Being a lizard, akin to the fish of the streams more than to us, it actually ate the flesh of the animals and men it killed. When it could get no living thing to eat, it chewed and swallowed leaves or grass, or the flowers and fruits of the trees. It had to. If it did not eat, it would die. It was too low in the evolutionary scale, it seems, to live as all warm-blooded creatures do, on the fresh water and fresh air that are free to all.

Because of this vile habit of eating, it always gave me a feeling of pleasure to kill these lizards whenever I could, almost like what the others boasted of when they came back from a raid and told of the fun of killing the members of the Enemy Tribe.

Four times in every year I was sent out to kill a lizard –

we called them Eaters – and each time I remained away until I caught one. Though it might take me days or weeks to track one down and slay it, I dared not come back without at least one skin on my shoulders. Though they became increasingly scarce, I always managed to trap one eventually – always, that is, but once.

For there finally came a day when, look where I would, use whatever arts of searching I knew, there was no Eater to be found. I ranged a hundred miles and more, over a period of nearly a month, utterly without success. In our own area of the planet, at least, the Eaters seemed completely extinct.

As I trudged into the village of my Tribe I saw that something was up. I had no wish to attract attention, since my quest had been fruitless, so I did not quite enter the village, but stood within the shelter of the trees and watched for a little while. The warriors were stalking around importantly in a bustle of scurrying women and hunters like myself, each warrior lugging a twelve-foot war bow.

A raid?

It had to be that. Little Clory, my favourite girlfriend, spied me before anyone else and came running up to me with a finger on her lips. 'Stay back, Keefe,' she warned. 'They're going out to lick the Red-and-Browns and you'd better not get in the way.'

I picked her up and sat her on my shoulder. She was a little thing, even for her seven years of age, but her long yellow hair covered my face. I blew it aside, and said, 'When will they have the Affair, Clory?'

'Oh, right away. Look – they're building the fires now.'

They were. The warriors had gathered and were seated in the triple-tiered Balcony of Men, while the youths and women built a tottering little shack of firewood. I should have helped them, being a non-military, but I wasn't needed, and I preferred to keep as much as possible out of anything connected with raids.

The whole Tribe was in the little clearing on the outskirts of the village by now. The House of the Enemy – that was the little jerry-built shack that would be burned – was nearly completed. The four braided vine ropes that would serve as fuses were already laid out, and the musicians were tuning up with an ungodly din.

Corlos, Chief of the Warriors, and Lord of the Tribe of the Blues, strode into the centre of the cleared circle, and raised his bow. A ten-foot arrow, hollowed at the point, was in it; he drew it back in the string until I could almost hear the wood of the bow creaking, then released it, aiming at the tiny red disc of the sun, setting on the horizon. The arrow screamed up and out in a flat arc – literally screamed, because the pitted point caused it to whistle in flight.

That was the signal. The musicians, who had been silent for a few moments, waiting their cue, screamed into their instruments, slapped their drums, sawed their stringed gourds. The noise was frightful – but almost beautiful, I had to admit. Maybe the beauty lay in the unusualness, because we heard this ceremonial music only just before a raid, not more than once in a year.

To the tune of the tempestuous music, a group of the younger girls of the Tribe came pacing in to the centre of the ring, bearing a closed palanquin on their shoulders. In it presumably, was the Enemy, the animal – sometimes, the person – which would be burned alive, representing the members of the Tribe against whom our warriors would soon be marching.

Corlos strode up to the car and halted, raising his arm peremptorily. The music stopped. In a savage, deep guttural he declaimed: 'Who is our Enemy?'

The antiphony rose in unison from the benches of the warriors: 'He who does not serve the Tribe – he is our Enemy: he must die! That which kills one of our Tribe – that is our Enemy; it must die! He who profanes the Name of our Tribe – he is the Enemy; he must die.' I repeated the familiar words of the Three Evil Acts with the warriors. I knew them by heart. Corlos went on with the ritual.

'How dies our Enemy?' he bellowed.

'By the flames of our fire,' rolled back the response.

'Where seek we our Enemy?'

'In the woods; in our Tribe; on mountains or plain; wherever he may flee, there we shall go.'

Corlos was working himself up to a frenzy. As the echoes of the warriors' shouts died away, he signalled to the musicians. A drum then boomed to accent each syllable, as he shrieked, 'Behold our Enemy!' He ripped open the door of the palanquin; four warriors ran up and dragged out the Enemy.

I stared hard, then stepped back a pace and clutched a vine for support. The Enemy, this time, was human. It was a youth, slight, shaking in a hysteria of fear. It was Lurlan, my sworn blood brother!

Lurlan! Except for Clory, I had rather see anyone of the Tribe perish in the flames, even myself, rather than him. Clory clutched my arm, and a tiny whimper escaped her. It was a surprise to her too, it seemed.

I dismissed the thought that I was on ground none too secure myself, and my mind spun as I tried desperately to think of a way of saving Lurlan from the flames. But there was no time for thinking, for in a matter of minutes the fire would be lighted and Lurlan's corpse would roast in its embers.

If he had to die, he would die. Certainly I could never hope to save his life. But – need he die in the horrible agony of the flames?

He did not, I decided agonizedly – and found that while I had been painfully thinking it out, my body's reflexes had come to the same conclusion. My bow was in my hands, and an arrow was notched. I took hasty aim and released the bowstring. The arrow fled from me and cleaved straight to its target – the throat of my blood brother, Lurlan.

Consternation! The entire Tribe was in an uproar. I saw proven then what I had always known – Corlos, though a beast and a braggart, was no coward. He whipped around like a pinked Eater, and peered directly at me, his slightly nearsighted eyes blinking in the smoke of the smaller fires. I could have slain him as easily as I had Lurlan, and he must have realized that. But he stood his ground, though his swarthy face turned pale and he fingered his arrowless bow.

'Keefe!' he bellowed as soon as he identified me. Then he spun back and faced the warriors. 'This man has slain the Enemy!' he howled. 'He has profaned the Tribe – he is our Enemy! Let us burn him!'

They had every intention of doing it, too. The warriors rose, howling with rage. Though none of them loved Corlos unduly, they were all hogtied with respect for the sacred traditions of the Burning of the Enemy. I had violated them. I was the Enemy.

I plucked at Clory and backed away, as unobtrusively as I could. I had my bow still in my hand; I notched another arrow and held it ready. I wanted them to see that I wasn't going to burn without a fight.

The bush was pretty thick, and within twenty feet we were hidden. Then I slung the bow over my shoulder and made speed with Clory.

'Where are we going, Keefe?' Clory mumured in my ear. She was obviously being as brave as she knew how. I didn't have to tell her that we were in serious trouble. Maybe if her own father hadn't been dead, killed in a raid while unsuccessfully trying to protect her mother, she would have made a fuss about going away with me. But the only person she was really close to in the Blues was myself. She trusted me, and that was a powerful incentive, because her own life might not be entirely safe if we were captured.

I could hear them shouting back in the clearing, howling for my blood. Then Corlos' bullish yowl sounded over the others; I couldn't make out what he said, but it seemed to quiet them.

I set Clory down on the ground and led her along. It was growing late. If the warriors were to raid the Red-and-Brown Tribe this night, they must leave soon, too soon to try to capture us – until they returned. That gave us a certain period of grace.

We stood statue-still for a second, listening for sounds of

pursuit. There weren't any. Apparently the Tribe had decided to let our punishment wait until the raid had been completed, for I could hear the chant of the warriors resume their deep-voiced promises of catastrophe to the Enemy Tribe.

Distantly Corlos' yowl came to me. 'So burns the Enemy!' he shouted, over the thin pounding of the drums. 'So dies their Tribe! Burn, Red-and-Browns! Burn with the House of the Enemy!' And there was a blood-freezing screech from fifty throats, as the warriors echoed, 'Burn!'

Then the drums rolled up to a bleak crescendo and stopped. I wondered what they had substituted for us in the House of the Enemy. Lurlan's corpse, probably. Well, better than his living body, or ours. I strained my eyes in the direction of the village, and saw the trees weirdly black and orange in the flickering of the burning shack. Then the cries died down and there was no sound we could hear, for a long time.

2

The Glider

I woke up with a start and clutched at my bow. Some sound had awakened me. Voices!

We had slept for hours, much longer than I'd intended. As I looked at Clory I realized that, for there was light to see her sleeping form. Dawn was near.

I rose cautiously without waking her, and peered around for the source of the voices. It was a party of warriors swinging along the trail, not twenty feet away.

Were they pursuing us? I saw they were not. They were pilots, the men who, secure in the speed of our gliders, would fly over the village we were to raid, shooting into the forces of the Enemy, dropping blazing torches if they could, causing disorder in a hundred ways. They were on their way to the hill where our gliders were kept, there to launch them and be on their way to the Enemy town.

I knew how to pilot a glider, that was one of the things for which I had been indebted to Lurlan. If we could steal one of those ships...

The men had passed out of hearing. Quickly I woke Clory and explained to her what I had seen, and the plan I'd made. Most wonderful of seven-year-old girls that she was, she understood immediately and followed me cautiously through the underbrush to the clearing where stood the catapults for the gliders.

We were noiseless – literally – as we wormed our way towards the clearing. We moved slowly, and as we approached we heard the dull 'dwang-g-g-g' of the released catapult as the first glider took to the air. We hid under a tree as it soared down the slope of the hill to gain speed, directly overhead. Luckily, the initial effort to gain altitude made it necessary for the pilots to cover a good deal of territory; they couldn't, therefore, wait for each other and proceed to the Enemy village *en masse*. If they had, our hopes of escape would have been ruined, for we would have been spotted immediately, and shot down.

I've never stalked an Eater as soundlessly as I led Clory, crawling, to the catapults. The sky was already showing colour, and the ground was wet with pre-dawn mist. I heard the catapult drone its fiddle note again – that was the second glider. Two gliders, each carrying two men, were gone; three gliders and eight men, if I'd counted correctly, were left.

A third glider had taken off before we gained the position I wanted, commanding the catapults. I counted the men in the clearing. There were five; I'd made an error before, but it was all to the good – it meant one man less to take care of later.

It seemed hours before the fourth glider was off and the time it took the three men remaining to wind the catapult again was weeks. But finally it was done.

I have said that I am a good marksman. Though I had always had a horror of killing men, the thought of what would happen to Clory and me if I weakened strengthened my resolve; as fast as I could speed the arrows, the three men dropped, one after another, and Clory and I broke for the glider. We fastened ourselves securely and I yanked on the release cable. There was a dizzying surge of motion and the loudest sound I ever heard, as the catapult arm threw us far out and up into the sky. We were free and away!

Clory had never been in the air before – few women or girls had. Her exuberance was unbounded as we skimmed on our way. I felt joyous too. It was a wondrous morning.

Morning is the best time for gliding, because there are all sorts of convection currents caused by the rising of the sun. I pushed over the lever arm to send us down in a flat glide for the riverbank. There was a small formation of cliffs there, big enough to send us a needed up-current. We reached it easily, and I spun the glider in a slow spiral as we climbed. We gained hundreds of feet of altitude before I levelled out, and headed in a straight line for the mountains to the North.

The flight was uneventful. Almost automatically I took the lift from every up-draft under a cloud. We weren't going really fast – I've run faster – but we were making steady progress over forests and swamps and rivers. There was only one fly in my ointment. I was tired – had had no sleep to speak of, and I certainly couldn't sleep while we flew. Yet we could land only one way: permanently, since we had no catapult.

My drowsiness grew and grew, as the miles slid by us. I had no particular destination; I steered by my shadow in front of me, cast by the morning sun behind. Though I kept reminding myself to stay awake, I drowsed again and again, each time coming a little closer to falling completely asleep and thus losing control. If only we could have landed for a second...

I suddenly realized that Clory was tugging at the back of my coat. 'Keefe!' she was crying urgently. 'Look!' I thrust off my sleepiness and turned to her smiling.

But there was a real alarm in her eyes as she pointed out

over the forests, and my smile died when I saw what she had seen.

It was another glider and it was flying straight for us.

In my amazement I nearly lost control. One of the other ships from our Tribe – it had to be that. Though it was a mile away or more, between me and the sun, it was much higher than we were and was coming at us impossibly fast, faster than I'd ever seen a glider go.

I had only one course – to flee. Cursing savagely, I dipped our craft until it was just skimming along the surface of the trees, fast as we could go.

But not nearly fast enough. The other glider was catching up with us as easily as we were overtaking the motionless trees ahead.

I wondered briefly how it had attained the altitude that gave it such speed from its initial dive, then turned all my attention to the controls.

Clory was holding to my coat with fervour. I could feel her body shaking with sobs as we both leaned forward, trying to cut down air resistance. I clung on to the controls tightly, fighting with all my energy for an extra foot of altitude, a trifle more speed.

A peak of green whipped up at us – crack! The ship jolted and faltered. I darted a glance below; we'd struck the top of a tree. Our landing skids had been wrecked.

But that had been the last of the tall trees; the land ahead sloped gently down. As far ahead as the eye could see was this gentle slope, the valley of an immense river bed. I tilted the controls and we picked up a few precious feet of speed in the shallow dive.

But our pursuer was faster yet. I glanced behind for a split second and saw it ominously close, close and huge. Much larger than our ship, it seemed...

'Clory!' I cried tensely. 'Can you fly this for a minute?' She didn't answer, but twined her arms around my neck and grabbed the levers. 'Good girl,' I muttered, unlimbering my bow. 'Just hold them that way for a second.'

I twisted under her arms and took careful aim at the

plane which followed us. I strained the bowstring back as far as I could and released it.

But Clory moved, just at the wrong moment! The cord struck her arm, the arrow was deflected far to one side. She gasped and winced from the cutting blow of the cord, and she must have jerked involuntarily at the controls.

For the ship's dive became abruptly steep and we spun crazily, whirling rational thoughts from my brain. I clutched at whatever I could reach; it turned out to be the control lever, killing our last chance of keeping to the air. The ship careened and fell off on to one wing, diving directly into a giant tree – the solid trunk of it, this time. I had time to realize before my face smashed into the hard, rough wood that little Clory had been thrown out of the glider. Then I struck!

I don't know how long I was stunned. I was cut and bleeding and my face felt raw when I came to, lying sprawled on a grassy mound. But no bones seemed to be broken. I leaped to my feet, crying Clory's name. If we could find shelter somewhere! The glider wouldn't dare to make a landing to scout for us. We might yet escape.

Clory did not answer. I dashed madly about, peering into the undergrowth, searching behind every bush. Then I spied her slight, white form lying motionless on the ground. I raced to her, fell to the ground beside her and shook her roughly.

She was unconscious – but not dead. My ear pressed to her heart convinced me of that. I tugged her to a sitting position...

And a shadow swept over me. I stared up. It was the other glider. We were seen.

Shaking Clory to bring her back to consciousness wasn't much use, though I tried it. The only thing I could do was to leave her there and run. The pilot of the glider, I hoped, would think she was dead. If I could hide long enough to make him give up hope of shooting me from the air...

The glider had whirled away; I could see its tail twist as the pilot banked it in a long curve, planed smoothly back towards us. I gaped no longer. I jumped to my feet and raced for cover.

I don't think I've ever run any faster than I did that dozen yards to shelter, but it seemed slow. Time passes slowly when you are expecting a five-foot arrow to feather between your shoulder blades.

But I made the cover, which was a long thicket of flower-ferns. Their broad leaves over me were perfect protection.

I knelt and glared up at the glider which was continuing its swooping back and forth. The sun was high now, and pouring into my eyes, so I had difficulty in seeing through the gaps in my roof. But I could see well enough to know that the flyer was something out of the ordinary.

It had seemed huge when we were fleeing from it, larger than I had ever seen a glider before. But now, when I could sit back and stare at it, I found that it was something brand new to me. It was no glider of our Tribe's, that was certain. Too large by far, designed much differently, with wings little larger than our own, but an immense fuselage slung low between the wings, twice as long as an ordinary glider.

It was made of something that shone and glistened in the sunlight. And it had a curious whirling contraption on each wing, something I'd never seen before, and could not understand. It flew low overhead, and I stared up at it. The pilot's face was visible over the side of the ship; so close that I could make out the features. It was no member of the Tribe. The face was surmounted by a headdress whose pattern was also unfamiliar to me.

I slumped back on the ground to think this over, and...

...Rose again much more rapidly, clutching a stung rump. I spun around and peered to see what had stung me. It was an arrow! I looked again and saw my bow, just outside the cover, lying temptingly exposed in the open.

I shot a quick look at the mysterious glider. The pilot was completing another arc, about to return. I leaped up and scuttled out from the flower-ferns, clutching the arrow. The bow was unharmed by its fall; I fitted the arrow to it, drew it back and took aim. The glider was sweeping closer, travelling at great speed, difficult to hit. But I'd never get a better opportunity – I stretched the arrow back as far as I could – released it!

There was a sharp note from my long bow, and I saw the new glider waver ever so slightly in its course. I'd hit it. I heard the voice of the pilot in a shout of pain and anger, saw him rise from the seat and try to leap clear as the ship sliced through the air in a whistling wingover, turned and plunged out of sight. I heard a loud splintering sound of breaking branches, and the crash of the ship, and a scream.

The hunter had been snared!

3

The Two from the Boat

Even after Clory had come to again, and was perfectly fit for travel, we two remained in the neighbourhood of where the strange ship had crashed. Somehow, in its fall, a fire had been started. How, I had no idea. Possibly there was a fire in the ship all the time, though that seemed unlikely. But there it was, an immense column of white-hot flame, almost invisible in the sunlight, shooting high at the heavens.

Clory and I watched it for some time without saying a word. We wanted to come nearer and investigate, but the flame was hot as well as bright. We sat on the banks of a river nearby and stared at the column of fire.

'What is it, Keefe?' whispered Clory, but all I could do was shake my head.

The ship twisted and moved in the heat of the pyre. Odd noises, almost human, came from it; they could have been the cries of the trapped pilot, but I thought that unlikely – they continued too long. Cracklings and sighings were to be heard for hours.

The sun began to set while we were still there. Luckily the ship had crashed in a clearing so there were no branches overhead to catch fire: the oddly long-lived flame expended its heat and light harmlessly in the air.

But not too harmlessly, I realized swiftly. Though it was still not completely dark, we could see the light of that hundred-foot flame, reflected from every tree in sight. What a beacon it was, visible for miles around.

I touched Clory's shoulder, and she followed me back, down the sloping banks of the stream and into the water. We waded as far as we could, then swam the hundred yards or so of the width of the stream. Just within the woods on the other side I spread small branches and grass on the ground, and covered the mass with my jacket. We would camp there for the night – it was as good a place as any.

All I had been able to salvage from our glider, except for my bow and arrows, was a short hunting knife. And I had only three arrows left. I determined to try to make some.

Clory fell asleep while I stripped the bark and leaves from a pair of straight, thin branches, then proceeded to whittle them down with the knife. I was no weapon maker, I discovered ruefully, but I managed to get the shafts smooth and straight as an arrow need be. I had yet to feather them though, and that wouldn't be easy. Nor would the job of getting bone or rock points for them.

I stopped whittling suddenly and cocked an ear. What was that? A whirring noise, faint but clear.

Without awakening Clory, I rose and stole noiselessly over to a point of better vantage, a knoll on the riverbank.

The origin of the muted sound was difficult to trace in the warm, dark night, particularly with the crackling of the huge flames across the river interfering. But it seemed to come from the river itself, at some point downstream from me.

The river was not broad, but it was straight as a lance, almost as though man-made. I could see a long way up and down it, at least a mile.

But I didn't have to see nearly that far. Much less than a mile away – a fifth of that, at most – was a group of moving lights, speeding up the river in my direction. As it approached I could see a dark hulk surrounding the lights, the shape of a ship. The whirr became louder.

But how did it move? Already it was close enough for me to see that it had no sails or paddles, nor was there a rope connecting it to anything on the bank which might be towing it. And it was moving much too rapidly for any of those methods to be responsible.

The connexion was obvious, and alarming. Whoever had been in the glider had friends – friends who, seeing the flame of its crash-pyre, had come to investigate.

Possibly they would not be inimical. I couldn't afford to find out. The thing for Clory and me to do was to get away from there.

But it could do no harm to linger for a while and see what would happen; we were safe, across the river.

Clory awoke and stole up beside me, slipping her hand into mine. Together we watched the strange craft dip in towards the riverbank next to the still-blazing ship.

The boat must have been of very slight draught, for it swung in within five feet of the beach before it halted. Light flared briefly on the shore as a door opened on the side away from us. The door closed again, and we saw two figures limned against the light of the fire as they climbed towards the ship.

They seemed scarcely human in the firelight, those two men. Certainly their dress was unlike that of any Tribe I knew. As they strode up the hill, all I could see was their backs, each wearing what seemed to be a species of bow slung athwart his shoulders. There was a criss-cross affair of belts on their backs, from which depended small objects that I couldn't quite define.

Clory's fingers gripped mine fiercely. 'Keefe!' she whispered piercingly. 'In the woods – over there. Look.'

I looked – and my shoulder blades crawled to meet each other. There was something huge and dark moving in the woods, shambling slowly towards the fire. It was an Eater – but a monster. Twenty feet long? More, much more.

The men did not see the approaching beast. They were regarding the blaze intently. One of them drew something out of a pocket – I could not see it clearly – and hurled it into the fire. Immediately the flame shrank; it was going out.

The Eater had come into the open now, but behind the two men. They could not see it. Should I shout and warn them, exposing myself if they were inimical? Or should I keep quiet and thus possibly condemn them to death?

Clory settled the question. Impulsively she raised her head and shrieked a warning to them across the stream.

The two men whipped around – and saw the Eater. I had to admire them for their quickness of thought – there was only a split second of hesitation before they recovered, and advanced on the Eater. Advanced on him – those two tiny men, unarmed as far as I could see.

Although, if their weapons were of as high a standard as their gliders and their boats, they might not be in any danger at all.

Their smooth efficiency was joyous to behold. In unison they unslung the short sticks I had thought to be bows and held them as you might a javelin. They were not more than four feet long – did the men hope to get close enough to run them into the huge animal?

They did, for they ran towards the Eater, divided, and as though following a carefully rehearsed programme, ran around the slow-thinking Eater. He turned to snap at one of them with his immense jaws – the one farthest from us. I could not see what happened, but I heard a yell of a man in agony which told me the story.

But the other man gained the position he wanted. He stabbed his javelin-like pole into the Eater's side. This time it was the monster that screamed in pain. Immense, fat sparks of light shot from the pole where it went into the creature's flesh. There was a high ripping sound, audible even at this distance, and I could feel for the Eater – that pole was deadly!

The squall of the wounded Eater drowned out other sounds, but the man must have cried out too. He had reason to, for the wounded monster, shuddering in unbearable agony, curled its huge length back upon itself and lashed out with its mighty tail. The tiny tip of it alone hit the man, but it was enough to flick him into the still-burning ship.

I think the man was dead before he began to burn. I hope so.

The Eater was dying too. As Clory and I watched, it staggered weakly off into the darkness, but could not even make the edge of the little clearing. It slumped to the ground, trembled all over once more, then lay quiet.

We watched, but nothing more happened. The two men had failed in their mission. They were as dead as the man they had come to save.

We decided, Clory and I, to reswim the river and see if there was any sign of life in the two men. With the death of the Eater, there was no other danger there, unless another beast had been attracted by the sounds of combat. That seemed unlikely, for an Eater as big as this would surely have killed or driven off all lesser ones.

We emerged dripping wet and walked quickly up the gentle slope. The men were dead – very. I reached the bodies before Clory, and I shooed her away. Every Tribe girl had seen death, Clory as much of it as any, but no seven-year-old girl had any need to see a corpse as ghastly as that of the man who had been slashed in two by the fierce jaws of the Eater.

The light of the fire was dimming – that little object the man had tossed in the flame was slow, but it did the work. As we watched, the fire grew less and less.

But it was not owing exclusively to the work of the man. Clory called my attention to that. 'Can we get somewhere out of the rain, Keefe?' she asked, shivering.

I started and looked around. Sure enough, it was raining. Pouring. It was out of the question for us to remain exposed to that downpour – already the fierce flame of the ship was out, though the wreckage was still too hot to approach. The question, of course, was where to go.

There was a dull booming crash from afar. Thunder. I could see the play of lightning flashes off in the distance. If the rain had already arrived, the lightning would soon be overhead. It would be very unpleasant to be near trees then.

Clory pointed – I followed her gaze. The boat! A very good place to be, undoubtedly. It had a roof – that was all we could ask. We ran down to it, tugged open the door, and stepped right in.

We closed the door tight behind us before we looked around.

And the first thing we saw was – them.

A man – and a girl. Dead, it seemed, for they lay unmoving, not even breathing. I stared at them. Neither was dressed in the odd garments of the two we had seen die. Their garb was much like our own, the everyday dress of Tribespeople.

'They must have been nice people,' Clory said aloud, and I found myself agreeing with her.

The man had as open and honest a face as any I've seen, and the girl was beautiful.

I stepped around them to get a better look at the girl's perfect features. They were lovely from any angle. I knelt to touch her pulse, and as my hand touched her wrist I felt a numbing tingle in my own fingers. I drew back my hand quickly.

There was a pale, bluish light falling on the two bodies from a lamp of sorts that hung over them. From the lamp extended a cord, which ran along the ceiling, then down the wall, terminating in a pedestal-like affair at the front of the boat, on which were dozens – hundreds! – of mysterious levers and dials. I moved over to examine it.

The levers were of all shapes and colours. I knew the purpose of none of them, but what harm could they do?

There was a temptingly small, red lever set into the very base of the pedestal. So small, and so far down, it could not be dangerous. 'Don't touch it, Keefe!' Clory's terrified voice begged as I stooped to finger it.

But I had already moved it.

Without result.

Emboldened, I moved another, then several more.

And with a lurch, the boat shuddered underfoot! The whirring sound again became audible, and it began to move. I had started it!

'Oh, Keefe! Why...'

But Clory stopped – words were of no use. I'd done it.

Together we raced for the door, staggering with the motion of the ship. It wouldn't open. Somehow the motion of the ship also controlled the door; I couldn't budge it. I leaped to a window and hammered on it. It just would not open, nor could I shatter it, though I shouldered it with all my weight behind the lunge.

Could I stop the ship? I turned back to the pedestal and stared anxiously, tempted. But which lever was the right one? I had no way of knowing, and I dared not experiment again.

I glanced out of the window fearfully. The angular prow of the ship divided the water into two neat curling crests, one on either side. The lightning had come, was striking at the taller trees all around. The black water ahead and the fierce play of light in the sky made a frightening combination.

'At least,' I said to Clory with a confidence I did not feel, 'we're going someplace. See how the boat stays in the middle of the river – something must be directing it. We'll be all right.' How could the boat be steered? I didn't know; certainly we were not steering it, nor was anyone else in the ship. Just one more mystery to tuck away in our minds.

I half heard a rustle of movement behind me, and turned to see that the 'dead' man had come to life again – dangerously!

He was creeping up to me, preparing to spring. If he had, it would have been a hand-to-hand fight, which I might have lost; he was powerfully built, and I had no time to draw my knife. But when he got a good look at me he faltered.

'Who are you?' he whispered, relaxing his menacing attitude.

'You're a Tribesman!'

The girl was alive too, I saw thankfully. She had been close behind him, backing him up.

4

The Mad Tunnel

Yes, we were Tribespeople, and so were they. We were all equally ignorant of the nature of the owners of the vessel in which we were. We exchanged stories.

Their adventures were interesting, but not very helpful. They, with all of their Tribe, had been asleep one evening. (Their Tribe was called the Greystripes – I'd heard of it, but it was too far away from my own village for us to have had any dealings, commercial or martial.) The girl's name was Braid; the man's, Check. Their individual huts were at almost opposite ends of the village; how they came to be together they did not know. They had gone to sleep in their own huts, and wakened, for a brief period, in a dimly lighted cell, together with dozens of other Tribespeople, all in an unnaturally deep sleep. They'd tried to arouse others, and failed. But their activities had drawn the attention of a guard dressed like the men Clory and I had seen, who had come in, found them awake, and pointed something long and tapering at them. They'd gone back to sleep, quite involuntarily, and awakened in the ship.

Our own story, which we then told, took more time. In fact, before we'd finished it, it was halted by an outside event. Braid had been keeping watch on the progress of the boat, and she suddenly cried out, pointing. The river forked off ahead, one branch continuing on into the distance, the other ending in what seemed to be the side of a mountain. Closer inspection revealed a hole, a tunnel, in that cliff wall; into it the boat unerringly sped, not abating its speed.

And a few seconds later the ship halted. The subdued whirr of the motors diminished and died altogether. There was a soft jar from outside and we were motionless. I seized the door; it opened freely.

The four of us crowded around the door and peered out cautiously. Not a living soul was in sight. After a moment, we stepped out, timorously at first, then more bravely, as it became evident that we were in no immediate danger.

Unless we wanted to entrust ourselves to that boat again, allowing it to proceed as it would back down the river – if, indeed, we could get it to move – we were trapped here. We might have been able to swim out, but it was a considerable distance; just how far, the darkness made it impossible to say. And there was no way at all of walking back through the tunnel, for the water lapped precipitous walls, except at the landing where we stood.

Set into the face of the rock there was a door, ajar. With one accord, we entered it.

We found ourselves in a long tunnel, which swept in a broad curve away from us in either direction. No human was visible, even now, though the place was brightly lit. Too brightly lit. It showed things that I could not understand, that drove me almost to the sharp brink of madness.

Picture a tunnel, a long one, and high and broad as well, descending in a shallow slant into the ground, as far as you can see. Fill it, in your mind, with a tremendous number of strange and eerie machines of some sort, each in motion. Make sure that every machine is different from the one next to it, and remember that each gives forth some tiny sound all blending together into a low, sustained chord, in which you can nevertheless distinguish individual tones.

Imagine that you are part way into the tunnel, that no human being is visible save three as ignorant as you, that the motions of the wheels and cams and levers of the machines are totally incomprehensible; see with amazement that in some cases there are wheels revolving in thin air, without an axle; that occasionally a piece of one machine will detach itself, float unsupported through the air to another, where it joins on, then recommences its spinning, twisting, gyrating activity; that more than once a wheel will roll completely through what appears to be a completely solid machine, leaving no hole or mark to show where it had entered.

Add to all this the fact that the machines are constructed of strange materials, some transparent, almost invisible, others seemingly transparent but curiously reflective; most of glistening metals – which, you must remember, you have seen comparatively seldom in your former life.

To our left, the tunnel sloped up, and downwards to our right. Up would mean the surface – but the entrance of the subterranean canal was in the direction of our right. Which way would take us out?

We spent minutes in debate, and could not decide. Braid settled it finally. 'When you cannot follow your head,' she said, 'you must follow your heart. We can try the left. If it seems the wrong way, we'll come back.'

So the four of us executed a broad left-wheel, and marched along that glittering action-filled tunnel. The machines – as I should have said – lined the walls only. The centre was a broad, flat path for us to walk on.

We walked mostly in silence, all of us gaping at the mad activity that surrounded us. For some distance we walked, until I tore my attention from the machines long enough to note that Check was acting strangely. He was twisting around to stare back, then forward; then tilting his head to peer at the ceiling overhead. A frown of puzzlement was appearing on his face.

'What is it?' I asked.

'I don't know – listen.' We listened, but heard nothing more than the constant machine-drone; the same drone we had been hearing all along.

But with a difference? Yes, surely. There was a new, growing note in the symphony. A deep buzz, something like the whirr of the ship's motors.

Check peered over his shoulder, and his face changed. He cried out and shoved my shoulder, spinning me around. I looked – and staggered.

Bearing down on us faster than any Eater ever ran was an

immense, wheeled metal shape. The noise was coming from it, from the sound of its huge wheels on the flooring, and from the hidden motor within. The thing was large – it almost filled the tunnel from top to bottom, though it wasn't wide enough by far to interfere with the machines that whirled along at the sides.

Leaving Check to look after Braid, I dragged Clory by main force into the maze of machinery at the side of the tunnel. We dodged spinning wheels and bars and climbed behind the pedestal of one of the machines.

Braid and Check were quick to do the same, but on the other side of the passage. But not quite quick enough, it seemed. Before they were well concealed, the metal monster was upon us. And it became evident that we had been seen.

For the thing squealed to a halt fifty feet beyond us, then rolled back to where we were and stopped.

5

The Subterranean City

I shouldn't have been surprised at the black cloud of sleep that descended over us all just then, because Check and Braid had told me about it before. I knew the people in that car were the same as the people who had abducted my two friends, but in the shock of that swift blotting out of consciousness, I didn't connect their experience with the present one.

Clory awakened me, and I found myself in a pleasantly light and cheerful room, lying on a luxuriously soft couch. We might be prisoners, but we were being treated well enough.

All four of us were there. For no reason except, perhaps, that she was the youngest and best able to throw off the effects of the sleep ray or whatever it was, Clory had come to first, and immediately roused me.

Together we woke Braid and Check.

The oddest feature of the room was its very curious windows. As we looked out of them from the interior of the room, we saw a blue sky with occasional puffy clouds. But as we approached, and tried to look down, the apparent transparency of the glass clouded. By the time one reached the window, it was almost opaque; only vague formless shadows could be seen. And as one walked away, the sky slowly reappeared.

The door, we found, was locked.

The style of the room's furnishings was far less strange than we might have imagined. Except that each item was so beautifully made, it might almost have been a Chief's home of any progressive Tribe.

But we didn't have too much time to investigate it. Some signal must have been given of our awakening, for the door flew open, and a man entered.

He seemed friendly enough, but when we besieged him with questions he said nothing, just stood there looking at us. There was no malice in his stare, but neither did he seem particularly interested.

He just stood there, regarding us. He was dressed like those of his kind we had already seen: the abbreviated divided trousers, tunic, belted back. In his hand he carried a smaller version of the rod we had seen used on the Eater; on his head he wore a flat-topped pillbox hat.

As moments passed without a movement from him beyond his shifting glances, Check edged over to me, darting meaningful stares at the man and at me. I didn't comprehend his meaning at first, but the stranger did.

'I wouldn't do that,' he said smoothly, and raised the rod a trifle. (Check and I both noticed for the first time that we were unarmed.) He continued his easy stare as Check brought up sharp, flushing.

'No,' said the man after a space, reflectively, 'I don't think you'll find it necessary to gang up on me. Certainly' – he gestured with the rod – 'you wouldn't find it safe. If you are all comfortable, we had better get started. There has been a special meeting of the Council to consider your problem. Come with me.' And he stood aside. But he would not answer questions even then, just gestured wordlessly with the rod.

You might think we could have overpowered him. Certainly it would seem that we could have – and should have – made some objection to going so freely with him. I thought so. I even attempted, in passing, to clutch at the door and slam it on him as he stood in the threshold, barricading ourselves in until we could make more definite plans.

But I couldn't. Just couldn't. My muscles would not obey the orders from my brain. It was like a complete paralysis, though I was perfectly free to walk, to look around, to do anything that did not conflict with his orders.

It was his pillbox hat that did it. There was a tiny instrument in it which acted to amplify his will, to force his commands upon others. Our thoughts he could not control, but our actions were his to command.

So we went with him quite obediently. We had not far to go, just out into a door-studded hall, and along it for a few feet until we came to an empty door. We entered, the door closed and we looked around perplexedly. We were in a tiny room, scarcely large enough for us. There was no furniture save a row of studs set in a wall by the door. This could not be our destination.

Nor was it. The man with the helmet stabbed one of the buttons with his forefinger and an inner door whirred shut. There was a muffled click, then the floor surged up under us, and the whole room shot up into the air.

There was a frightened squawk from Clory, who grabbed me and hung on. I was nothing much to cling to, having left my stomach below when the room swooped up, nor were the others in a better state. The man took it calmly enough, grinning at our discomfiture, though, so I concealed my apprehension as much as I could.

The motion lasted only a few seconds. Then it stopped smoothly and the door opened. We were escorted out and into a large, handsome hall.

The man with the rod escorted us in, then stepped aside.

'This is the Council Chamber,' he said. 'Go forward and answer the questions of the Council.'

We stepped forward timorously, and he made his exit. The Council Chamber was vast – larger, even, than the big ceremonial field back in the village of the Tribe, the field in which I was nearly burned to death. How long ago that seemed!

A triple-tiered balcony ran around the wall. It reminded me of the Balcony of Men back in the ceremonial field, though the crude wooden balcony there was not to be compared with this ornate structure of metal and fabrics. The seats were occupied, with some vacancies, by perhaps fifty men and women. They eyed us with much the same friendly unconcern that had characterized the man with the rod.

We were brought up before this impressive audience and seated in chairs as comfortable as their own. The questions began almost immediately.

The oldest of the Council – they were a youngish lot – rustled some papers on the flat arm of his chair and glanced at us piercingly. 'Have you any objection to allowing Check to act as your spokesman?' he asked suddenly. Check asked us with his eyes; we all nodded.

'None,' he said. 'But how did you know my name?'

'I know a great deal about you – all of you,' laughed the judge. 'Braid and Keefe better than Clory, and you best of all, but even Clory is familiar to me. We have heard of her from her father.'

'Her father!' I gasped as Clory squealed in surprise. 'Her father is dead!'

'No. Clory's father is not dead. He is – elsewhere, just now, but he is alive. Perhaps Clory may see him soon, when he returns. At the time of his "death" he was injured by a blow. He did not die, but he would have, had not one of our patrols found him. When he was well again we examined him, as we are examining you now, and decided favourably... But we will do the asking here, just now. You, Check, tell me: how did you come to be here?'

Check told what he knew, and I supplemented the account with Clory's history and mine. The interrogator appeared to be satisfied; when he had finished, he held a low-pitched conversation with those around him, which we could not hear. For a few moments all of them talked among themselves, then apparently a decision was reached.

The one who had questioned us signed to a guard standing by the entrance, who opened the portal and admitted three men trundling a large, flat box on wheels, from which depended flexible tubes of varying descriptions. The guard, who was wearing one of those hypnotic hats, accompanied them up to us, ordering us to do as they said.

We submitted perforce to having a tube wrapped around the wrist of each of us, various other gadgets clamped to other parts of our anatomy, and our eyes bandaged so we could see nothing. As soon as all the equipment was adjusted to their satisfaction, one of them commenced to question us.

But what questions! Nothing we could have expected – at least, not in our right minds. Apparently they had no desire to learn facts, to discover what we wanted to do here, or anything about our backgrounds. To the accompaniment of ominous buzzings and clickings from the machine, we were asked such questions as, 'If you were to be imprisoned in a dark room for twenty-four hours, what would you do?' and, 'Would you prefer to witness a pageant or take part in it?' and others even less rational. I could hear a stylus scratching the answers on a pad, and wondered what type of persons these might be.

Then I heard a cry of alarm from Braid and tensed my muscles to rip off my blindfold and see what was happening. I couldn't, of course; the hypnosis of that helmet forbade any resistance. But I felt a gentle pressure in my arm, and then a stinging jolt of mild electricity. I leaped, and I think I cried out too. A squeal from Clory and a grunt from Check showed that they had received the same treatment.

Our blindfolds were removed, but the tests continued. They detached all the gadgets from Clory and sent her away to sit in the corner, while Braid, Check and I were quizzed in a new fashion. A string of such words as 'read', 'learn', 'sleep', 'eat', and other verbs of varying meaning were spoken to us, and one of the men noted the readings of a leaping dial needle attached to the bands on our wrists.

But that was all. We were released from the apparatus and conducted out of the room by the same man who had brought us. As we left, the head man of the Council called to us, 'You will return tomorrow, and everything will be clear. Have patience till then.'

We were returned to our room, where we found ourselves unaccountably sleepy. Though we had been awakened not more than four hours before, we could not stay awake. We sought couches and lay down. Just as I was dropping off. I thought I saw the door open, and a man enter and fasten something to Clory's head. It appeared to be a helmet, but I could not force myself to awaken and make it out. As he approached me, I dropped off into deep slumber.

6

The Dream

My sleep was full of dreams – odd ones. I saw myself in a thousand impossible situations.

Quite naturally, I dreamed of the scene in the Council Chamber. But in the dream I was not the object of the Council's attention – I was a member of it. In fact, I was Chief of the Council. Before me, in one fantasy of sleep after another, were brought dozens of persons to be asked the questions I had been asked that day; thousands of other persons with other problems to be settled. I could not understand the tenth part of those problems, but in my dream I knew all about them; I solved them all, to the complete satisfaction of everyone. I was not supreme among the Council, but I was its coordinator, the one finally to resolve each knotty problem according to the suggestions of the others.

As the dreams grew in clarity, an immense amount of background material began to fill it. I saw a teeming, populous world, many times the size of my own. Almost completely underground, it was, but it filled millions of square miles on a hundred different subterranean levels. In this new world – which I came to identify with the underground city my sleeping body was in – was a complete civilization, vaster by far than all the Tribes put together, of a culture and depth of understanding that bewildered me.

The surface of this world, I saw, was given over to relaxation. No one died, either on the surface or below, save by accident, but the swift pace of the underground life aged its inhabitants, made them old in mind while still young in body. They needed refreshment, refreshment which meant a complete relaxation, complete forgetting of all the cares of the world below. Forgetting, even, that there was a world below...

At which point I awakened. It was morning again – according to the elusive sky on the window – and the others were awakening too.

They had had much the same sort of dream, with individual differences. Check had dreamed of himself, not as leader of the Council, but as a worker in a sort of 'large room, with funny pieces of machinery spread all over', as he described it. He seemed to have been engaged in some sort of research, but he did not know any more about it. Clory had not seen herself in any of the dreams. Braid hesitated, looked fearfully disturbed about something, then finally said she couldn't remember, and stuck to it.

Eventually the guard came once more and took us out again to go to the Council.

In the elevator, I saw something that took me a moment to comprehend. The guide carried the force rod, and seemed as supercilious, as free from worry about our actions as ever – but he did not wear the mind-compelling hat! I stared again to make sure, then nudged Check to a position behind the man and pointed. Check saw, widened his eyes, then together we whirled on the man and bowled him over.

Our muscles obeyed us! The man cried out, then lashed at us with arms and legs, but our first leap had knocked the rod from his hands. It was two against one, and Check and I were strong. The man toppled to the floor, Check upon him; I secured the rod and turned it on him.

Just then the elevator door commenced to open quietly – we had arrived. And as it slid open, we all saw just outside a full dozen of armed men walking along the corridor!

I was staggered, but had presence of mind enough to level the weapon at the foremost of them. 'I'll kill the first one to move,' I yelled, and meant it – it simply never occurred to me that I didn't know how to operate the thing!

The men outside didn't know that. It was an impasse.

Braid caught Clory to her instinctively and said, 'What shall we do, Keefe?' I didn't know, but I could not afford to have either her or the men know that.

I asked a question. 'Do you think you can run that car?' I didn't take my eyes off the men, but I could se her shadow at the little bank of keys.

'Maybe – not very well,' her voice came. 'At least I think I can start it.'

That was not so good. 'Check – come here,' I called after a space.

He stirred suddenly, as though my command had jolted him out of some deep thought. He stepped slowly forward, still with puzzlement at something in his eyes, and looked a question at me.

'Take the rod from one of them,' I ordered, stabbing my weapon at one of the men. He hesitated. 'Go ahead,' I cried with irritation. 'There may be more along in a minute.'

He hesitated for only a second after that. Then, with a swift swoop, he snatched a rod, stepped back a pace – and snatched my rod!

Swinging it to cover all of us, Clory and Braid and me as well as the men, he wrinkled his brow. 'Now, wait a minute, all of you,' he muttered. 'I want to think—' He stared at the men, and at us, then shrugged. 'Get up!' he cried to the original owner of the rod. 'I'm going to see this through. We're going to the Council Chamber!'

The man rose, smiling. 'You are coming along very well,' he observed cryptically, and led the way along the hall. Nor did he say anything more.

The man whom, in my dreams, I had replaced as leader of the Council, widened his eyes in surprise as the lot of us entered. 'Weapons?' he murmured questioningly. 'There should be no weapons in here.'

But Check said, 'I am not sure of that, yet – though I am beginning to believe it. But I shall keep this until you explain things to me.'

The man smiled. 'There is no need to explain,' he said, seating himself. I saw with a start that he had not taken the seat of the day before, but was in a small, less conspicuous seat to one side of it and below. That was how I had dreamed it!

'No,' repeated the old man, 'there is no need to explain any more. We have explained already. Did you not have dreams last night? ... Yes. Those dreams, then, were fact. We induced them, hypnotically, to tell you what words could not tell as well.

'If you had accepted them as fact, they would have told you that this city is your home. Your real home, more so than the Tribes from which you came. Even, it is Clory's home, though she was born in a Tribe. Her father and her mother lived here.'

'This snake hole?' ejaculated Braid.

The man laughed gently. 'This is not all of the world. This city here, which houses a paltry few thousand people, is only one of a hundred thousand such; the others all on other planets. This world is merely the sixth satellite of the fifth planet circling one sun. And each of the other planets is inhabited, and many planets of other suns. On the third planet of the sun is the home of our race, from which we all stem, but there are a thousand times as many people of our race now as the planet could hold – even were there still Death.'

'But why—' I began, and then stopped, for the man had raised a hand.

'I shall tell you the "whys" in a moment,' he said. 'And when I have told you a few of them, to prepare you for the shock, your minds shall be returned to you.'

Check quickened his breath at those words. His rod dropped unnoticed to the floor; one of the men picked it up and slung it over his shoulder. Before we could ask another question, the old man went on.

'As I have said, there is no more Death, save by accident. You know that; you know that, though many disappear, few die. Those who disappear come here.

'For immortality brings age. The fine blade of the mind dulls from constant use. The body does not sicken nor age, but the mind grows old. It must be rested.

'And for that are these rest planets – one in every System – established. All knowledge, save of the simple art of language, walking, and the others, is taken from a man when he is discovered to need rest. He is given an artificial, hypnotic memory, and sent to join a Tribe. For a dozen years or more he lives with the Tribe, while his mind grows younger. Then he is brought back, as were Check and Braid, or finds his way back as you did. And he takes up his place again, refreshed.'

He paused and looked sharply at the door. It was open; a man was entering, bearing a shimmering bright gem in his hand. 'You have all been examined,' he continued slowly, 'and found to be completely rejuvenated. Then you were given the sleep-teaching treatment, to prepare you, and then this little speech. You are now ready to have returned to you your full minds, with all the memories of your long, long lives!'

The man with the crystal stepped forward, looking from one to the other of us. 'Keefe will be first,' said the older one. 'Simply look into the jewel.'

I looked – I heard the man who carried it commence to speak, a droning voice that compelled sleep. In seconds the voice faded away, and the lights dimmed and the entire world was dark. Then there was a sound like thunder, and I heard the words, 'Awake!'

My eyes opened, and I felt a maddening, dizzying swirl of thoughts into my brain. I reeled and clutched at the man as my brain, stung into swift activity, sorted and filed the knowledge it had taken me a long lifetime to acquire.

I stood there, swaying. Then there was a sudden feeling of released tension, and I opened my eyes.

Everything suddenly, was familiar. I knew my life, and what I had to do.

And with a sort of joyous gravity I had never known in the life of the Tribe, I stepped forward and, with the ease of long experience, slid quietly into the seat of pre-eminence among the Council.

UNDER TWO MOONS

I

THE BOLT OF flame from the sun hissed by, twenty millimetres from his nose.

There was silence, and then the door opened behind him. Light footsteps approached, muffled by the fine, deadly dust on the floor. Gull craned to see the person approaching, but he was tied too tightly for that.

'You are most foolhardy, Meesta Gull,' said the girl's soft voice. 'I beg you, do not drop the fuse again or I must resort to more 'arsh methods.' And from the corner of his eye Johan Gull saw her slim figure swiftly stoop to recover the half-metre length of rubbery plastic fuse cord.

As she attempted to jam it into his mouth again he jerked his head aside and managed to ask, 'Why are you doing this?'

'Why?' There was the soft hint of a laugh in her voice. 'Ah, why indeed!' She caught his head in the crook of an arm and, surprisingly strong, held it still. He felt the stiff strand thrust between his teeth, tasted again the acrid chemical flavour. When she had done the same thing before, he had been able to spit the fuse out before she could ignite it. She did not chance his dropping it again; her flame gun hissed, and the end of the fuse began to sizzle with a tiny green spark.

'I think,' she whispered, 'that it is because I love you, Meesta Gull.' And he felt something like a quick touch of lips, a scent of perfume that carried even above the pyrotechnic reek of the sputtering fuse; and then the door closed softly and he was alone in the room that was about to become an enormous bomb.

The green halo hissed the length of the dangling fuse towards his lips. Johan Gull, estimating seconds by the beat of his pulse where his wrists were tied to the wall, timed its course at perhaps two millimetres a second. Say four minutes before it reached his lips.

He sighed. It was a nuisance to think of his career ending like this – a daring foray into enemy territory to break up a smuggling operation of the Black Hats – complete success, the ring destroyed, the dozen men in charge of it dead – and then to allow himself to be tricked by the one person who survived, a slip of a girl. If he had only not answered her cry for help!

But he had. And he had found himself trussed up in a karate grip, then tied to the wall. And now – he had four minutes of life, or actually a bit less, unless he thought of something rather quickly.

He could, of course, drop the fuse at any time before the spark touched his flesh and his instinctive reaction made him drop it. But the girl had said, and he had no reason to think that she lied, that the powdery dust she had spread about the floor was gunpowder. In the unconfined space of the room it would perhaps not explode; it might only flare up like the igniting of a gas jet; but it would kill Johan Gull nonetheless. Could he scrape a spot clean with his feet and drop the burning fuse there?

Experimentally he shifted position and tried. It was slow work. The floor was rough-cast cement and the tiny particles of explosive powder adhered like lint on wool. By arduous scraping with the side of his shoe Gull managed to get a six-inch square mostly free of the stuff. But it was not good enough, he saw. A pale powdery haze clung to the crevices. It was not much, but it was too much; it would take very little to flash and carry the spark of the fuse to the main mass; and two minutes were irretrievably gone.

Could he sneeze it out? It was at least worth a try, he thought; but annoyingly his nose would not itch, there was no trace of nasal drip, all he managed to do was snort at the tiny green light and make it flare brighter for a moment.

He redoubled his efforts to slip his wrists out of their bonds. The thing could be done, he discovered with tempered pleasure. The girl had tied him well; but she was only a girl and not strong enough, or cruel enough, to cut deeply into his wrists. The cord stretched slowly and minutely; he would be able to work himself free.

But not in four minutes. Still more certainly not in the minute or less that was all he had left. Already he could feel the heat of the glowing end of the fuse on his chin. He was forced to lean forward for fear of igniting his goatee, but soon it would be too close for that to help.

There really was only one thing to do, thought Johan Gull regretfully.

He nibbled the short remaining length of fuse up to his lips and, wincing from the pain but denying it control of his actions, chewed out the spark.

A quarter of an hour later he was free of his bonds and through the door.

The girl was long gone, of course. Spirited little devil. Gull wished her well; he bore her no animus for taking one round of The Game, wished only that he had been able to see her more clearly, for her voice was sweet. Perhaps they would meet again.

Rubbing his wrists, Gull looked about the dingy shed in which he had been held captive. He knew this part of Marsport less well than almost any of the rest of the red planet, but recognized this rundown corridor as a slum. An uncollected trash basket kicked over on its side spewed refuse across the steel decking. On the black wall that had housed him some despairing wretch had scrawled, *We Are Property!* The air pressure was low, but it reeked of dirt, drugs and vice.

Gull shrugged, lit a cigarette, turned his back on the room that had so nearly been his death trap and strode towards the sign marked *Subway*. He would be late, and .5 was a stickler for promptness. But he paused to glance back again, and thought of the girl who had trapped him.

He had liked her voice. She had had a charming fragrance. It had been cool of her to have ignited the fuse while she was still in the room; he might have dropped it and then and there blown both of them halfway to Deimos. And she had said that she loved him.

2

The entrance to Security lay through a barber shop. Gull hung his coat on a rack and sat back in the chair, musing about the adventure he had just had and wondering about the next to come. In the corridor outside a chanting mob of UFOlogists demanded equal rights for spacemen; Gull had nearly been caught in the marching front of their demonstration as he entered the shop.

He submitted to being lathered, shaved, talced and brushed, but the jacket he was helped into was not his own. His hand in the pocket closed over the familiar shape of the pencil-key. He let himself out the back way of the barber shop and opened the private door to .5's office.

'Sorry I'm late, sir,' he apologized to the ancient leathery figure with the hooded eyes behind the desk.

The Old Man's secretary, McIntyre, looked up from his eternal notebook. From the hooks and slants in that little leather-bound pad messages flew to every corner of the Solar System, alerting a battalion of Marines on Callisto, driving a Black Hat front into bankruptcy in Stuttgart, thrusting pawns against a raid on Darkside Mercury, throwing an agent to his death here on Mars. To McIntyre it was all the same. He was a dark young man who had never been known to show emotion. He said calmly, '.5 is a stickler for promptness, Gull.'

Gull said, 'I ran into difficulties. Something didn't want me to get here today, I'm afraid.'

Was it his imagination, or did .5's imperturbable face show the vestige of a frown? McIntyre put down his pencil and regarded Gull thoughtfully. 'I think,' he said, 'that you'd better tell .5 just what you mean by that.'

'Oh, just that I had difficulties, sir.' Quickly Gull sketched the events of the day. 'Afraid I allowed myself to be decoyed. Shouldn't have, of course. But next thing you know there was a flame pencil in my ribs, I was tied up and had a lighted fuse between my teeth. Quite unpleasant, as the floor was covered with gunpowder. I would have been here sooner, but I didn't quite trust myself to spit the fuse clear of the gunpowder.'

Eyebrows raised, McIntyre glanced at .5, as if to find a sign on that stoic countenance. Then he rose deliberately, walked to a file, pulled out a sheaf of papers in a folder marked, *Gull, Johan, Personnel Records of*. He glanced through them thoughtfully.

'I see,' he said at last. 'Well, that's neither here nor there.' He replaced the folder and sat beside Gull. 'Johan,' he said earnestly, '.5 wants me to caution you that your next assignment may mean unusual danger.'

'Really, sir? Oh, delightful!'

'More than you think, perhaps,' said McIntyre darkly. 'It isn't merely our colleagues in the Black Hats this time. It's mob hysteria, at least. Perhaps something far more sinister. Something's up in Syrtis Major.'

After fourteen years as an agent and innumerable hearings of those words, or of words very much like them, still a thrill tingled up the spine of Johan Gull. *Something's up in Syrtis Major* – or Lacus Solis. Or the Southern Ice Cap. And he would be off again, off in the gratification of that headiest of addictions, the pitting of one's wits and fine-trained body against the best the other side could come up with.

And they were resourceful devils, he thought, with the journeyman's unselfish admiration for a skilled worker at his own trade. Time and again it had taken all he possessed to win through against their strength and tricks. And if .5 felt it necessary to caution him that this coming exploit would be trickier than usual, it would indeed be something to remember.

'Smashing,' he cried. 'Would you care to brief me on it?'

But McIntyre was shaking his head.

'If you'd managed to get here on schedule—' he said; and then, 'As it is, .5 has some rather urgent callers due in, let me see, mark! Forty seconds.'

'I see,' said Johan Gull.

'However,' McIntyre went on, 'Research has the whole picture for you. You'll draw whatever supplies are necessary in Supply. Then Travel & Transport can arrange for your travel and transport. Goodbye, Gull.'

'Right, sir,' said Gull, memorizing his instructions. His lips moved for a second and he nodded. 'Got it. So long, McIntyre. Goodbye, sir.' He did not wait for an answer. It was well known that .5 disliked wasting breath on trivia, above all on the conventional exchange of greetings and farewells and unmeant inquiries as to the important aspects of one's health that passed for 'politeness'.

In the office these perfunctory pleasances were skipped. Gull let himself out, his heart pounding in spite of himself, and started towards the Research office and a new job.

It was rather a nuisance, thought Gull as he lay sprawled in the barber's chair, to go again through the process of being lathered, shaved, talced and brushed. But it did have advantages. One advantage was that it gave one a moment to onself now and then.

Johan Gull was a healthy young animal. He had an educated interest in food, drink and the attractions of women; a moment for reverie taken perforce, like this, was a luxury – the sort of luxury his active body was inclined to deny him when it had a choice. He dreamed away the moments, hardly hearing the barber-robot's taped drone – 'How you think the Yanks gonna do? Say, you see this new *raggazz'* on the TV last night? Hoo!' – while his mind roamed the ochre wastes of Syrtis Major. He thought contentedly that he was ready for the assignment.

The jacket he was helped to put on bore on its cuff a quite unduplicable pattern of metal-linked lines and dots. Gull climbed the winding stairs down to the basement of the barber shop, held the sleeve to a scanning device and was admitted to the Research centre.

Lights, sounds and activity smote his senses. He blinked, pausing on the threshold of the room as the great steel door swung soundlessly closed behind him.

As it never failed to do, the busy hum of Research thrilled him with a sense of the vast massive scope of Security's incredibly complex operations. The chamber was more than thirty metres across. It was in the form of an amphitheatre, with circles of desks descending towards the great central dais. There on a pivot, its axis inclined an exact 24° 48′ from the vertical, the great globe of Mars majestically turned, its cities and trafficways and canals etched out in colours that were softly glowing or startlingly bright. Here a rhythmic green flash pinpointed one of Security's agents on active duty. There a crimson warning signal winked the presence of a known enemy operative. Patches of blue and orange indicated areas of military build-up or of temporary calm; white flashes showed Black Hat strongpoints under surveillance; .5's own bases were gold.

Any Black Hat field man would gladly have paid his life, and a bit more, for five minutes inside the Research chamber. It was the most secret installation in all Security's vast net. In it, any of three hundred trained technicians seated at their rows of desks on each step of the circle could look up and, in a moment, identify a trouble signal, record a 'mission accomplished', demand and get a dossier on any adult Martian citizen or guest, or put into operation any of .5's magnificently daring ventures. And what was most impressive about it all, thought Gull, was that this infinitely detailed accumulation of expertise was duplicated in full in one other place – in the fecund convolutions of .5's busy brain.

Gull observed that the appropriate face of Mars was towards him now. He quickly sought the lines of the canals, followed them to Syrtis Major, paused and frowned.

The whole mass of the area was glowing with a pale lavender radiance.

Gull stood puzzled and faintly worried, until one of the girls at the circling desks rose and beckoned him. As he approached she sat down again and waved him to a chair. 'Good afternoon, Mr Gull,' she said. 'One moment until I get your account records.'

Gull grinned, more amused than otherwise. 'Oh, come off it, Gloria,' he said easily. 'I know I was a stinker last night. But let's not hold grudges.'

She said stiffly, 'Thank you for waiting, Mr Gull. I have your records now.'

Gull's smile did not fade; he had observed the faint softening of the corners of her mouth. 'Then let's get to it,' he said genially.

Her fingers had been busy on the console. A faxed sheet emerged from a slit on the lip of her desk and she read it carefully, nodding.

'Ah, yes. I thought so,' said the girl. 'It's that flying saucer affair in Syrtis Major.'

Gull's smile vanished. He smote his brow. 'Flying saucers! Of course.' Comprehension overspread his face and he nodded. 'Saw the lavender on the globe, of course, but I must admit that for the moment I forgot my colour-coding. Couldn't remember that it meant flying saucers.'

The girl was looking at him ruefully. 'Oh, dear,' she sighed. 'Johan, you've just earned yourself a one-hour refresher. You know .5's a stickler for keeping colour-coding in your head.'

Gull groaned, but she was adamant. 'No use fighting it. It'll do you good, dear. Now about this flying saucer thing.'

She glanced over the faxed sheet to refresh her memory, then spoke. 'About two weeks ago,' she said, 'a couple of old mica prospectors reeled in off the desert with a story about having been captured by strange, godlike creatures who landed near their camp in a flying saucer. There's a transcript of their stories on this tape' – she took a spool from a drawer of her desk and handed it to Gull – 'but essentially what it comes to is that they said these creatures are so far superior to humans that they consider us to be domesticated animals at best.'

'Have the same feeling myself from time to time,' said Gull, pocketing the spool.

'I know *that*, dear. Anyway, nobody paid much attention. Not even when the prospectors swore they'd been given the power of walking through fire without being burned, putting themselves into catalepsy, even levitating themselves. However, then they began doing it in front of witnesses.' She took another spool of tape from her desk, then two more.

'This one's synoptic eyewitness accounts. This one's a report from Engineering on possible ways that these phenomena may have been faked. And this other one's a rebuttal from Unexplained Data, covering similar unexplained phenomena of the past forty-odd years.'

'Keep an even balance, don't we?' grinned Gull, pocketing the spools.

'For God's sake, Johan, don't get them mixed up. Well, anyway. About half of Syrtis Major decided the prospectors were fakes and tried to lynch them. The other half decided they were saints, and began to worship them. There's a whole revivalist religion now. They think that the saucer people own us...'

'Oh, yes,' said Gull. 'I know about that part.' Indeed, it was hard not to have seen some of their riotous, chanting mass meetings, to dodge their interminable parades or to have failed to observe the slogans they had painted all over Marsport Dome.

'Then you won't need these other tapes.' Gloria sat back, frowning over her checklist. 'Well, that's about it, th...'

A bright golden light flashed on the girl's desk.

In the middle of a word she stopped herself, picked up the scarlet hushphone marked *Direct* and listened. She nodded. 'Right, sir,' she said, replaced the phone, and made a quick notation on the fax sheet before her and returned to Gull.

'...en,' she finished. 'Any questions?'

'I think not.'

'Then here are your operating instructions, submarine reservations, identification papers and disguise kit.' She handed him another reel of tape, a ticket envelope, a punch-coded card with a rather good likeness of an idealized Johan Gull on it and a bottle of hair colour.

Gull accepted them and stowed them away. But he paused at the girl's desk, looking at her thoughtfully. 'Say. Would you like me to take you home tonight?'

'Good heavens, no. I haven't forgiven you that much.' She made two check marks on the fax sheet. 'Anyway, you won't have time.'

'Why do you say that? My submarine doesn't leave for four hours...'

She smiled. 'That call was from .5's office.'

Gull said gloomily, 'Cripes. I suppose that means extra lines.'

'Absolutely essential you complete two one-hour refresher courses before leaving,' the girl quoted. 'McIntyre was quite emphatic. Said to remind you that .5 was a stickler for maintaining high levels of training: half-trained agents jeopardize missions.' Gull sighed but surrendered. No doubt .5 was right. 'What's the score?' he asked.

'One hour in colour-code recognition, but don't think I reported you. Probably .5's office was monitoring us. The other – let me see – oh, yes. Basic fuse-spitting, refresher course. Good luck, Johan. Drop me a card from Syrtis Major.'

Gull kissed her lightly and left.

He paused in the entranceway, studying his tickets and operating orders. He was faintly puzzled.

That in itself was all right. He remembered and liked the feeling. It was a good sign; it was the operations where one couldn't quite see the drift at first that often turned out to be the most exciting and rewarding. Yet he wished he knew how this mission was going to be.

He turned his back on the flickering darting lights that came from the great turning Martian globe and began to trudge up the stairs. All right, so Syrtis Major had got the wind up. Mass hysteria, surely. In itself, that sort of thing was hardly worth Security's while to bother with. There was no sign of the opposition's fine Machiavellian hand in it, less reason to believe that there would be real danger.

Yet McIntyre had warned of 'unusual danger'.

Surely he was wrong. Unless...

Unless, thought Johan Gull with a touch of wonder, as he sat back in the barber's chair and felt the warm lather gliding along his cheek, as the shoeshine-robot waited to pull the lever that would drop him into the chute to Plans & Training – unless there really *were* people from flying saucers on Mars.

3

Smells of fungi, smells of the sea. The tang of hot-running metal machinery and the reek of stale sewage. Johan Gull expanded his chest and sucked in the thousand fragrances of the Martian waterfront as he shouted, 'Boy! My bags. To my cabin, chop-chop!'

He followed the lascar-robot at a slow self-satisfied pace, dropping ash from his panatella, examining the fittings of the submarine with the knowing eye of the old Martian hand. He did indeed feel well pleased with himself.

In the role Costumery had set up for him, that of a well-to-do water merchant from the North Polar Ice Cap, he had arrived at the docks in a custom Caddy. He cast largesse to the winds, ordered up a fine brandy to his cabin and immediately plunged into a fresh-water bath. When you were playing a part, it was as well to play a wealthy one, he thought contentedly; and when he had luxuriated in his bath for fifteen minutes and felt the throb of the hydrojets announce the ship's getting under way, he emerged to dress and play his tapes with a light heart.

To all intents and purposes, Gull must have seemed the

very archetype of a rich water vendor of substantial, but not yet debilitating, age. He sat at ease, listening to the tapes through a nearly invisible ear-plug and doing his nails. He did not touch the eye patch which gave his face distinction, nor did he glance towards the framed portrait of Abdul Gamal Nasser behind which, he rather thought, a hidden camera eye was watching his every move. Let them damned well look. They could find nothing.

He sat up, stretched, yawned, lit an expensive Pittsburgh stogie, blew one perfect smoke ring and resumed his task.

The *T Coronae Borealis* was a fine old ship of the Finucane–American line. As a matter of fact Johan Gull had voyaged in her more than a time or two before, and he looked forward with considerable pleasure to his dinner that night at the captain's table, to a spot of gambling in the card room, perhaps – who knew? – to a heady *tête-à-tête* with one of the lovely ladies he had observed as he boarded. The voyage to Heliopolis was sixteen hours by submarine, or just time enough for one's glands to catch up with the fact that one had changed one's *mise-en-scène*. Ballistic rockets, of course, would do it in fifty minutes. In Johan Gull's opinion, ballistic travel was for barbs. And he was grateful that Mars' atmosphere would not support that hideous compromise between grace and speed, the jet plane. No, thought Gull complacently. Of all the modes of transport he had sampled on six worlds and a hundred satellites, submarining through the Martian canals was the only one fit for a man of taste.

He snapped off the last of the tapes and considered his position. He heard with one ear the distant, feminine song of *T Coronae*'s nuclear hydrojets. Reassuring. With every minute that passed they were two-fifths of a mile closer to the junction of four canals where Heliopolis, the Saigon of Syrtis Major, sat wickedly upon its web of waters and waited for its prey.

Gull wondered briefly what he would find there. And as he wondered, he smiled.

The knock on the door was firm without being peremptory. 'Another brandy, sir?' called a voice from without.

'No, thank you, steward,' said Gull. No Martian water vendor would arrive at dinner half slopped over. Neither would Gull – if not because of the demands of his role, then because of the requirements of good manners to the handiwork of *T Coronae*'s master chef. Anyway, he observed by his wrist chronometer that it was time to think things over.

He reviewed what he had heard on the tapes.

Those two prospectors, he thought. Damned confusing thing.

Their names, he recalled, were Harry Rosencranz and Clarence T. Reik. He had checked their dossiers back to pre-emigration days. There had been nothing of interest there: Rosencranz an ex-unemployed plumber from Fort Leavenworth, Kansas; Reik a cashiered instructor in guerrilla tactics from the nearby Command & General Staff School. Like so many of Earth's cast-offs, they had scraped together money to cover passage to Mars, and enough over to outfit one expedition. They had managed to subsist ever since on what scrubby topazes they could scratch out of the sands of the Great Northern Desert. With, thought Gull, no doubt a spot of smuggling to make ends meet. Duty-free Martian souvenirs into the city, and chicle for the natives out. So much for Harry Rosencranz and Clarence T. Reik, thought Gull, blowing gently on the second coat of polish and commencing to buff his nails to a soft gleam. But it was not who the prospectors were that mattered. It was what they had had to say – and above all, what they had done.

Gull paused and frowned.

There was something he could not recognize in the atmosphere. A soft hint of fragrance – tantalizing – it strove to recall something to him, but he could not be sure what. A place? But what place? A girl?

He shook his head. There could be no girl here. He put the thought from his mind and returned to the two prospectors and their strange story.

Their testimony far outran the parameters of normal credibility. Gull could repeat the important parts of what they had said almost verbatim. Reik had been the more loquacious of the two...

Well, Harry was like cooking up our mulligan outside the tent when I thought I heard him yell something. I stuck...

Q. One minute, Mr Reik. You couldn't hear what he said clearly?

A. Well, not what you'd call clearly. You see I had the TV sound up pretty loud. Can't hear much when you got the TV sound up pretty loud.

Q. Go on.

A. Well, I just reached out and turned off the set and stuck my neck out the flap. Geez! There it was. Big as life and twice as scary. It was a flying saucer, all right. It glowed with like a sort of pearly light that made you feel – I dunno how to say it, exactly – like, peaceful.

Q. Peaceful?

A. Not only that. *Good.* It made me sorry I was such a rat.

Q. Go on.

A. Well, anyway, after a minute a door opened with like a kind of a musical note. F sharp, I'd say. Harry, he thought it was F natural. Well, we got to fighting over that, and then we looked up and there were these three, uh, creatures. Extra-terrestrials, like. They told us they had long watched the bickerings and like that of Earthmen and they had come to bring us wisdom and peace. They had this sealed book that would make us one with the Higher Creation. So we took a couple...

Q. They gave you each one?

A. Oh, no. I mean, they didn't give them to us. They *sold* them to us. Twenty-five bucks apiece. We paid them in topazes.

Q. You each had to have a book?

A. Well, they only work for one person, see? I mean, if

it's anybody else's book you can't see it. You can't even tell it's there.

Gull frowned. It would be sticky trying to learn much about the book if one couldn't see it. Still, even if the book itself were invisible, its effects were tangible indeed – or so said the account on the tapes. Reik had described his actions on entering Heliopolis:

Harry he lemme his switchblade. I stuck it right through my cheeks, here. I didn't bleed a drop, and then I kind of levitated myself, and after a while I did the Indian Rope Trick, except since I just had my good necktie for a rope I couldn't get far enough up to disappear. You have to get like seventy-five per cent of your body height up before you disappear.

Q. Could you disappear if you had a long enough rope?

A. Hell, yes. Only I won't. You get to a higher cycle of psychic Oneness like me and you don't kid around with that stuff any more.

Q. Did you do anything else?'

A. Well, not till after dinner. Then I put myself in a cataleptic trance and went to sleep. I didn't do that any more after that, though. Catelepsy doesn't really rest you. I was beat all the next day, but I figured what the hell. I was still only on page seven.

Gull sighed, relit his stogie and contemplated the shimmering perfection of his nails.

And at that moment his doorchime sounded. Through the open switch of the announcer-phone came a sound of terrified sobbing and the throaty, somehow familiar voice of a frightened girl:

'Please! Open the door quickly, I 'ave to see you. I beg you to 'urry, Meesta Gull!'

Gull froze. He realized at once that something was amiss,

for the name on his travel documents was not Gull. Steadily he considered the implications of that fact.

Someone knew his real identity.

Gull called, 'One moment.' He was stalling for time, while his mind raced to cope with the problems that deduction entailed. If his identity were known, then security had been breached. If security were breached, then his mission was compromised. If his mission were compromised...

Gull grinned tightly, careless of the possible camera eye that would even now be recording his every move. If his mission were compromised the only intelligent, safe, approved procedure would be to return to Marsport and give it up. And that, of course, was what Johan Gull would never do.

Carefully, quickly, he slid into his socks and slippers, blew on his nails to make sure they were dry and threw open the door, one hand close to the quick-draw pocket in his lounging robe where his gun awaited his need.

'Thank God,' whispered the girl at the doorway. She was lovely. A slim young blonde. Blue eyes, in which a hint of recent tears stained the eyeshadow at the corners.

Courteously Gull bowed. 'Come in,' he said, closing the door behind her. 'Sit down, if you will. Would you care for coffee? A drop of brandy? An ice-cream?'

She shook her head and cried, 'Meesta Gull, your life is in 'ideous danger!'

Gull stroked his goatee, his smile friendly and unconcerned. 'Oh, come off it, my dear,' he said. 'You expect me to believe *that*?' And yet, he mused, she was really beautiful, not more than twenty-seven, no taller than five foot three.

And the tiny ridge at the hemline of her bodice showed that she carried a flame pencil.

'You must believe me! I 'ave taken a frightful chance to come 'ere!'

'Oh, yes, no doubt.' He shrugged, gazing at her narrowly. It was her beauty that had struck him at first, but there were more urgent considerations about this girl than her charms. For one thing, what was that she carried? A huge bag, perhaps; it almost seemed large enough to be a suitcase. For another...

Gull's brows came together. There was something about her that touched a chord in his memory. Somewhere – some time – he had seen that girl before. 'Why do you come here with this fantastic story?' he demanded.

The girl began to weep. Great soft tears streamed down her face like summer raindrops on a pane. But she made no sound and her eyes were steady on his. 'Meesta Gull,' she said simply, 'I come 'ere to save your life because I must. I love you.'

'Hah!'

'But it is true,' she insisted. 'I love you more than life itself, Meesta Gull. More than my soul or my 'opes of 'Eaven. More even than my children – Kim, who is six; Marie Celeste, four; or little Patty.' She drew out a photograph and handed it to him. It showed her in a plain knitted suit, with the three children grouped around a Christmas tree.

Gull softened slightly. 'Nice-looking kids,' he commented, returning the picture.

'Thank you.'

'No, really. I meant it.'

'You're being kind.'

Gull started to reply, then stopped himself.

For he was falling into the oldest trap in the business. He was allowing his gentler emotions to interfere with the needs of the assignment. In this business there was no room for sentiment, Gull thought wryly. Better men than he had been taken in by the soft passions and had paid for it, in death, in torture, in dismemberment – worst of all, in the failure of a mission. 'Hell with all that stuff,' he said gruffly. 'I still can't accept your story.'

'You must! The Black 'Ats 'ave a plan to kill you!'

He shook his head. 'I can't take a stranger's word for it.'

The tears had stopped. She gazed at him for a long, opaque moment. Then she smiled tantalizingly.

'A stranger, Meesta Gull?'

'That's what I said.'

'I see.' She nodded gravely. 'We 'ave never met, eh? And therefore I could not possibly know something about you – oh, something that perhaps is very private.'

'What are you talking about? Get to the point!'

'Something,' she continued, her eyes veiled but dancing with amusement, 'that perhaps you 'ave told no one else. A – shall we say – a sore lip, Meesta Gull? Received, perhaps, in an alley in the Syrian quarter of Marsport?'

Gull was startled. 'Really! Now, look. I – confound it, how could you possibly know about that? I've mentioned it to no one!'

She inclined her head, a tender and mocking gesture.

'But it's true! And there was no one there at the time! Not a single living soul but myself and the woman who trapped me!'

The girl pursed her lips but did not speak. Her eyes spoke for her. They were impudent, laughing at him.

'Well, then!' he shouted. He was furious at himself. There had to be some rational explanation! Why had he let her catch him off-balance like this? It was a trick, of course. It could be no more than that. There were a thousand possible explanations of how she could have found out about it— 'Well, then! How did you know?'

'Meesta Gull,' she whispered soberly, 'please trust me. I cannot tell you now. In precisely seven minutes' – she glanced at her watch – 'an attempt will be made on your life.'

'Rot!'

Her eyes flamed with sudden anger. 'Idiot!' she blazed. 'Oh, 'ow I 'ate your harrogance!'

Gull shrugged with dignity.

'Very well! Die, then, if you wish it. The Black 'Ats will kill you, but I will not die with you.' And she began to take off her clothes.

Johan Gull stared. Then soberly, calmly he picked up his

stogie, relit it and observed, 'Your behaviour is most inexplicable, my dear.'

'Hah!' The girl stepped out of her dress, her lovely face bitter with anger and fear. A delicate scent of chypre improved the air.

'This tactic will get you nowhere,' said Gull.

'Pah!' She touched the catch on her carrying case. It fell open and a bright rubbery coverall fell out, with mask and stubby, bright tanks attached.

'Good heavens!' cried Gull, startled. 'Is that a warmsuit? SCUBA gear?'

But the girl said only, 'You 'ave four minutes left.'

'You're carrying this rather far, you know. Even if there are Black Hats aboard, we can't leave the submarine underwater.'

'Three minutes,' said the girl calmly, wriggling into her suit. But she was wrong.

The submarine seemed to run into a brick wall in the water.

They were thrown against the forward wall, a Laocoon of lovely bare limbs and rubbery warmsuit and Gull entwined in the middle. A huge dull sound blossomed around them. Gull fought himself free.

The girl sat up, her face a mask of terror. 'Oh, damn the damn thing,' she cried, shaking her wrist, staring at her watch. 'I must've forgot to set it. Too late Meesta Gull. We 'ave been torpedoed!'

4

The warbling *wheep-wheep* of alarm signals blended with a confused shouting from the steerage holds below. The cabin lighting flickered, went out, tried once more, failed and was replaced by the purplish argon glow of the standby system. A racking, shuddering crash announced the destruction of the nuclear reactor that fed the hydrojets; somewhere, water was pouring in.

''Urry, Meesta Gull!' cried the girl.

'Of course,' said Gull, courteously assisting her with the warmsuit. He patted her shoulder. 'Not to worry, my dear. I owe you an apology, I expect. At a more propitious time...'

'Meesta Gull! The bulkheads 'ave been sabotaged!'

Gull smiled confidently and turned to his escape procedures. Now that it was a matter of instant action he was all right. His momentary uncertainty was behind him.

Coolly he reached into his pocket, unsnapped the little packet of micro-thin Standing Orders and scanned their titles. 'Let me see, now. Checklist for air evacuation – no. Checklist for enemy attack, artillery. Checklist for enemy attack, ICBM. Checklist for...'

'Meesta Gull' she cried, with a real fear in her voice. ''Ave you forgotten that these waters are the 'abitat of the Martian piranha? You must 'urry!'

'Well, what the devil do you think I'm doing? Now be still; I have it here.' And crossly Gull began to check off the items under *Submarine torpedoing, Martian canals*: Secret papers, maps, halazone tablets, passports, poison capsule, toothbrush, American Express card ... with metronome precision he stowed them away and instantly donned his own SCUBA gear. 'That's the lot,' he announced, glancing distastefully at the dirty froth of water that was seeping under the door. 'We might as well be off, then.' He lowered the SCUBA mask over his face – and raised it again at once, to fish out a packet of Kleenex in its waterproof packet and add it to his stores. 'Sorry. Always get a sniffly nose when I'm torpedoed,' he apologized, and flung open the door to the passageway.

A three-foot wall of water broke into the cabin, bearing with it a short-circuited purser-robot that hummed and crackled and twitched helplessly in a shower of golden sparks. 'Outside, quick!' cried Gull, and led the way through the roiled, tumbling waters.

The brave old *T Coronae Borealis* had taken a mortal wound. Half wading, half swimming, they fought strongly against the fierce drive of inwelling waters towards an escape hatch. In the dim purple gleam of the standby circuits they could see little. But they could hear much – shouts, distant screams, the horrid sounds of a great ship breaking up.

There was nothing they could do. They were lucky to be able to escape themselves.

And then it was nothing; a few strong strokes upward, a minute of clawing through the gelid, fungal mass that prevented the canals' evaporation and had concealed their water from Earthly telescopes for a hundred years – and they were safe. Armed and armoured in their SCUBA gear, they had no trouble with the piranhas.

Gull and the girl dragged themselves out on the bank of the sludgy canal and stared back at the waters, gasping for breath. There were ominous silent ripples and whorls. They watched for long minutes. But no other head appeared to break the surface.

Gull's face was set in a mask of anger. 'Poor devils,' he allowed himself, no more.

But in his heart he was resolved. A hundred men, women and robots had perished in the torpedoing of the *T Coronae*. Someone would pay for it.

Across the burning ochre sands they marched ... then trudged ... then stumbled. The pitiless sun poured down on them.

'Meesta Gull,' sobbed the girl. 'It is 'ot.'

'Courage,' he said absently, concentrating on making one foot move, and then the other. They had many miles to go. Gull's maps had indicated a nearly direct route from the canal along the Sinus Sabaeus where the submarine was slowly beginning to rust, straight across the great hot sweep of Syrtis Major to Heliopolis. A direct route. But it was not an easy one.

Step, and step. Gull thought sardonically of the two prospectors who had come out of this desert to start all the trouble. When they entered Heliopolis it had been on a magic carpet that slid through Mars' thin air like a knife. Nice to have one now, he thought – though exhaustive tests had shown the carpet itself to be a discontinued Sears, Roebuck model from the looms of Grand Rapids. But somehow they had made it work...

He sighed and called a halt. The girl fell exhausted to the sands.

'Meesta Gull,' she whispered, 'I cannot go much farther.'

'You must,' he said simply. He fell to studying his maps, checking the line of sight to the distant hillocks that passed, on Mars, for mountains. 'Right on,' he murmured with satisfaction. 'See here. Seven more miles west and we're in the Split Cliffs. Then bear left, and...'

'You are not 'uman! I must 'ave rest – water!'

Gull only shrugged. 'Can't be helped, my dear. But at least the sun will be behind us; now. We can do it.'

'No, no!'

'Yes,' said Gull sharply. 'Good God, woman! Do you want to be caught out here after dark?' He sneezed. 'Excuse me,' he said, fumbling a Kleenex out of the packet and wiping his nose.

'Five minutes,' she begged.

Johan Gull looked at her thoughtfully, dabbing at his nose. He had not solved the mystery she presented. There was every reason to be on guard. Yet she had truly warned him of the torpedoing of the submarine, and surely she could be no threat to him out here, as piteously weakened as she was. He replaced his breathing guard and dropped the Kleenex to the ground. A moment later the empty pack followed. It had been the last.

But Gull merely scuffed sand over it with his foot and said nothing; no sense adding to her worries. He said chivalrously, 'Oh, all right. And by the way, what's your name?'

She summoned up enough reserves of strength to smile coquettishly. 'Alessandra,' she murmured.

Gull grinned and nudged her with his elbow. 'Under the circumstances,' he chuckled, 'I think I'll call you Sandy, eh?'

'Don't jest, Meesta Gull! Even if we survive this trip, you 'ave still the Black 'Ats to face in 'Eliopolis.'

'I've faced them before, my dear. Not to worry.'

''Ave you seen what they can do now? With their creatures from outer space?'

'Well, no. But I'll think of something.'

She looked at him for a long and thoughtful minute. Then she said, 'I know you will, Meesta Gull. It is love that tells me so.'

5

Step, and step. In Mars' easy grasp a man can lift much, jump high. But to slog through desert sands is little easier than on Earth; the sliding grains underfoot rob him of strength and clutch at his stride. They were near exhaustion, Gull knew with clarity; and for the past half-mile the girl had been calling to him.

Gull closed his ears to her. He kept his eyes on his own lengthening shadow before him, even when he heard her sobbing. They had no strength to spare for conversaton.

'Meesta Gull,' she whispered brokenly. 'Wait, please.'

He kept on grimly, head down, feet moving like pendulums.

'Meesta Gull! But I must ask you something.'

Over his shoulder he murmured, 'No time for that, old girl. Keep walking.'

'But I 'ave to know.'

'Oh, for God's sake,' he said, and waited for her to catch up. 'What is it now?'

'Only this, Meesta Gull. If we are 'eading west, why is the sun behind us?'

'Really, Sandy! I swear you have no consideration at all!'

'I am most sorry, Meesta Gull. I only asked.'

'You only asked,' he repeated bitterly. 'You only asked! And now you know what I have to do? I have to stop and take out the maps and waste all kinds of time just to satisfy your damned curiosity. Of course we're heading west!'

'I really am very sorry.'

'And the reason the sun's behind us – well, if you knew

geometry – look here. I'll show you on the map.'

She fell to the ground again as he pored over the charts, frowning at the horizon, returning to his grid lines. At length his expression cleared.

'I thought so,' he said triumphantly. 'Perfectly simple, my dear. Up you get.'

With rough tenderness he helped her to her feet and set off again, smiling. She did not speak at first, but presently she ventured, 'Meesta Gull, we are 'eading towards the sun now. And these seem to be our own footprints we are retracing.'

Gull patted her good-humouredly. 'Don't worry, Sandy.'

'But, Meesta Gull . . .'

'Will you for God's sake shut up?' Confounded women, thought Gull. How they did go on! And he might have said something harsh to the poor girl, except that that occurred which drove all thoughts of compass headings from both their minds.

There was a terrible thunder of many hooves.

Alessandra whimpered and clutched his arm. Gull stopped short, waiting; and over a rise in the ocre sands came a monstrous grey-green creature with six legs. It was huge as an elephant and its look was deadly; and it bore a rider, a huge, manlike, green-skinned creature with four arms, holding a murderous-looking lance.

The thoat, for such it was, skidded to a stop before them. Its monstrous rider dismounted with a single leap.

For an endless second the creature glared at them through narrowed, crimson eyes. Then it laughed with a sound of harsh and distant thunder.

'Ho!' it cried, tossing the lance away. 'I won't need this for such as you! Prepare to defend yourself, Earthling – and know that you face the mightiest warrior of the dead sea bottoms, Tars Tarkas of Thark!'

The girl cried out in terror. Johan gripped her shoulder, trying to will strength and courage into her.

It was damnably bad luck, he thought, that they should

somehow have taken the wrong turn. Clearly they had blundered into private property – and he had a rather good idea of just whose property they had blundered into.

He stepped forward and said, 'Wait! I believe I can settle this to everybody's satisfaction. It's true that we don't have tickets, Tars Tarkas, but you see we were torpedoed in the Sinus Sabaeus and had no opportunity to pass the usual admission gate.'

'Wretched Earthling!' roared the monster. 'If I issue you tickets there is a ten per cent surcharge; I don't make Barsoomland policy, I only work here. What say you to that?'

'Done!' cried Gull, and amended it swiftly. 'Provided you'll accept my American Express card – otherwise, you see, I have the devil of a time with the old expense account.'

The creature bared yellow fangs in a great, silent laugh. But it interposed no objection, and the card was quickly validated by comparison with the Barsoomian's built-in magnetic file. Tars Tarkas nodded his enormous head, swiftly wrote them out two lavender slips and roared, 'Here you are, sir. If you wish to exchange them for regular family-plan tickets at the gate there will be a small refund ... I am assuming the lady is your wife,' he twinkled. 'And now, welcome to Barsoomland. Be sure to visit the Giant Sky Ride from the Twin Towers of Helium, in the base of which are several excellent restaurants where delicious sandwiches and beverages may be obtained at reasonable prices. Farewell!'

'I think not,' said Gull at once. 'Don't go. We need transportation.'

'By the hour or contract price?' parried the Martian.

'Direct to Heliopolis. And no tricks,' warned Gull. 'I've taken this ride fifty times. I know what the meter should show.'

Muttering to himself the creature leaped up on his thoat and allowed them to clamber behind. And they were off.

The motion of the thoat was vaguely disconcerting to the sense of balance, like a well-trained camel or a very clumsy horse. But it ate up the miles. And for a nominal fee. Tars Tarkas consented to supply them with food and drink.

Gull ate quickly, glanced at the girl to make sure she was all right – which she was, though a trifle green and apparently not greatly interested in food – and set to work to question the Thark. 'You've had some interesting goings-on,' he yelled up towards the enormous head.

'It is even so, Earthling,' tolled Tars Tarkas' great voice.

'Flying saucers and that sort of thing.'

The bright red eyes regarded him. 'Evil things!' roared the Thark sombrely. 'May Iss bear them away!'

'Oh, I certainly hope that too,' agreed Gull. He was hanging on to the Barsoomian's back, his face at about the level of the creature's lower left-hand armpit, and carrying on a conversation presented difficulties. But he persevered. 'Have you seen any of it yourself?' he asked. 'Psionics or any of that? UFOs? Little green monsters?'

'Watch your mouth!' cried the Barsoomian, enraged.

'No, no. *Little* green monsters. Nothing personal.'

The Thark glared at him with suspicion and hostility for a moment. Then the huge, reptilian face relaxed. The Thark muttered, 'Not now. When we get to Heliopolis, go to the...'

The voice broke off. Tars Tarkas cocked a pointed ear, and stared about.

With a whirring, whining sound, something appeared over the dunes. The girl cried out and clutched at Gull, who had little comfort to give her. Whatever it was, it was not of this planet – or of any other that Johan Gull had ever seen. It had the shape of a flying saucer. It glittered in the blood-red, lowering sun, arrowing straight towards them. As it drew near they could see the markings on its stern:

UFO Cumrovin 2nd
Giant Rock, Earth

'Blood of Issus!' shouted the Barsoomian. 'It's one of *them*!'

Tars Tarkas bellowed animal hatred to the dark Martian sky and raised his lance. Fierce white fires leaped from its tip – struck the alien vessel, clung and dropped away. The craft was unharmed.

It soared mockingly, tantalizingly overhead for a moment, seeming to dare them to fire on it again. Then a single needle of ruby light darted out of its side, reached down and touched Tars Tarkas between his bright red eyes.

The Barsoomian seemed to explode.

The concussion flung them from the thoat. Dazed, stunned, aching in every bone, Johan Gull managed to drag himself to his feet and look around.

The alien spacecraft was gone. The girl lay stunned and half unconscious at his feet. Yards away Tars Tarkas was a giant mound of grey-green flesh and bright metal parts, writhing faintly.

Gull staggered over to the creature and cradled the ravaged head in his lap.

The scarlet eyes stared sightlessly into his. The ruin of a mouth opened.

'We – are property,' whispered Tars Tarkas thickly, and died.

6

Once, when Johan Gull was very young, the newest and least reliable of cogs in Security's great machine, he had been assigned to Heliopolis to counter a Black Hat ploy. Or not quite that, he admitted; he had been sent to add a quite unimportant bit of information to the already huge store that the agent operating on the scene already had. He had envied that agent, had young Johan Gull. He had looked with jealous eyes about the bright dizzying scenes of Heliopolis and dreamed of a time when he too might be a senior agent in charge, himself a major piece in The Game, squiring a lovely lady on an errand of great consequence, in the teeth of dreadful danger.

All the fun of it was in the anticipation, he thought as

they rode into Heliopolis lock on their battered thoat, checked it at the Avis office and dismounted. If only Tars Tarkas had survived to tell what he knew!

But he had not; and Gull was uneasily aware that he knew no more now than when he left Marsport. Still, he thought, brightening, this was Heliopolis, the Saigon of Syrtis Major. He might get killed. He might not be able to protect this lovely and loving girl from mischance. He might even fail in his mission. But he was bound to have a hell of a time.

They found rooms at the Grand and parted to freshen up. Overhead the city's advertising display flashed on the thin, yellowish clouds of Mars, on, off – on, off:

HELIOPOLIS
The Wickedest City in the Worlds
Liquor * Gambling * Vice
The Family That Plays Together
Stays Together

And indeed, Gull saw, the pleasure seekers who thronged the concourses and the lobby of the Grand had often enough brought the kiddies. He watched them sentimentally as the bellthing trundled his luggage towards the elevators. It would be most pleasant to spend a holiday here, he thought, with someone you loved. With Alessandra, perhaps. Perhaps even with Kim, Marie Celeste and little Patty...

But he could not afford thoughts like that; and he quickly showered, shaved, put on a clean white suit and met the girl in the great gleaming cocktail lounge of the Grand.

''Ello, Meesta Gull,' she said softly, her eyes dark and somehow laughing.

Gull regarded her thoughtfully. She was a sight worth regarding, for the girl in the cocktail lounge was nothing like the bedraggled, terrified creature in the ochre sands. Her green-blue eyes were smoky with mystery. Her leong-sam, deeply slit, revealed the gleam of a bronzed rounded thigh. A whisper of some provocative scent caressed him; but it was not her charms that had him bemused; it was something else. His eyes narrowed. Somewhere, he thought. Some time . . .

She laughed. 'You are thoughtful,' she said. 'Will you 'ave a drink with me?'

'The pleasure is all mine,' he said gallantly.

'Unless you have other plans?' she inquired. There was no doubt about it; she was poking fun at him.

He rose to her mood. 'It's the least I could do, my dear – seeing you saved my life.'

'Ah! Life.' She glanced wryly at him from the corner of her eye. 'What is it, this "life" I 'ave saved? Can one taste it? Can one carry it to bed?'

Gull grinned. 'Perhaps not, but I'm rather attached to mine.' He ordered drinks, watched carefully while they were made, then nodded and raised his glass. 'Of course,' he added, 'I've saved your life too – I guess, let's see – oh, perhaps three times. From Tars Tarkas. From dying by thirst. From the saucer people. So you actually owe me about three to one, lifesaving-wise.'

'Three to two, dear Meesta Gull,' the girl whispered over the rim of her glass.

'Two? Oh, I think not. Just the torpedoing, really, and as a matter of fact I'm not sure you should get full credit for that. You *were* a little tardy there.'

She shook her head. 'Yes, the torpedoing – and something else. 'Ave you forgotten? The old warehouse? The – incident – which caused your sore lip?'

Gull stared at her, then brought his glass down with a crash. 'Got it!' he shouted. 'I remember now! . . . Oh, damn it, sorry,' he went on shaking his head. 'It was on the tip of my tongue, but I've lost it. Sorry.'

He stared at her moodily and drained his glass. 'No matter. I'll think of it. I promise you that.'

The girl laughed softly, then sobered. 'Meanwhile,' she said, 'we 'ave some more important business 'ere.' And she nodded towards the great crystal pane that opened on the thronged boulevards of Heliopolis.

Gull followed the direction of her glance and saw at once what she meant. A demonstration was in progress. A hundred straggling, shouting marchers were carrying placards with as many harsh and doctrinaire slogans:

Let the Space People Save You!
We Are Property
Why Is the Air Force Covering
Up Sightings?

Gull said abruptly, 'Let's take a look.'

The girl rose without answering and together they walked out to the terrace. The shouts of the demonstrators smote them like a fist. Gull could barely distinguish the cadenced words in the roar of sound: *'Make ... Mars ... the tomb of scepticism,'* over and over in time to their march until it changed to 'Welcome UFOs *now*! Welcome UFOs *now*!'

'They take it seriously,' he murmured. Alessandra did not answer; he glanced at her, then followed the direction of her gaze. A man in stained coveralls, eyes fixed on them, was pushing his way in their direction through the crowd. He was tall, and not young. His face was lined with the ineradicable burn of a life spent on the Martian desert.

Gull stroked his goatee to hide a thrill of excitement that tingled through him. This could be it: the break he was looking for.

The man stopped just below them, looking up. 'Hey, you!' he bawled. 'You Gull?'

Gull shouted carefully, 'That's my name, yes.'

'Well, where the devil you been? We been waiting for you!' cried the man in irritable tones. He reached up, clutched at a carved projection on the face of the terrace, raised himself and swung to face the crowd. 'Hey, everybody!' he shouted. 'Here's the fella that thinks UFOs are phoney! This way! You! Look here!'

Heads were beginning to turn. The ragged line of marchers slowed, Gull whispered to the girl, whose presence he could feel shivering beside him, 'Careful! I don't know what he's going to do. If it looks like trouble – run!'

But he could not hear her answer, if she made one, for the man was turning back to him again. In the diminished sound of the street his raucous yell sounded clearly: 'All right, Gull! You think our supranormal powers're all a lotta crud, see what you think of this!' And he made a snatching motion at what, as far as Gull could see, was empty air; caught something, squeezed it in his fist; turned towards Gull and threw it.

There was nothing in the man's hand.

But that nothing spun towards Gull like a pinwheeling comet, huge and bright and deadly; it hummed and sang shrilly of hate and destruction; it rocketed up towards him like an onrushing engine of destruction. And something in it sapped his will. He stood frozen, impotent to move.

Vaguely he felt a stir of motion beside him. Hazily he knew that the girl was thrusting at him, shouting at him, hurling him aside. Too late! The hurtling doom came up and struck him – just a corner brushing against his head as he fell – but enough; worlds crashed; hell-bombs roared in his skull; he dropped, away and away, endlessly down into – into – he could not see, could not guess what it was; but it was filled with terror and pain and doom.

But then he was awake again, and the girl was weeping over him; he could feel her teardrops splashing on his face.

Gull coughed, gasped, clutched at his pounding skull and pushed himself erect. 'What – what ...'

'Oh, thank 'eaven! I was afraid 'Arry 'ad killed you!'

'Apparently not,' he said dizzily; and then, 'Harry who? How do you know what that fellow was?'

'What does it matter?' she cried. Bright tears hung unshed in her eyes.

'Well it kind of matters to me,' said Gull doubtfully, looking around. They were no longer on the terrace. Somehow she had lugged him back into the greater security of the cocktail lounge. A waiter was hanging over them, whirring in a worried key.

'Harry Rosencranz!' he cried suddenly. The girl nodded. 'Sure! And he knew I was coming. Well, that tears it. My cover's blown for sure.' He glared at the waiter and said, 'Don't just stand there. Bring us a drink.' The thing went away, warbling unhappily to itself. It had not been programmed for this sort of thing.

Indeed Gull needed a drink. The reality of supranormal powers was a phenomenon of a totally different kind from the contemplation of them at a distance. The tapes about Reik and his partner had been interesting; the reality was terrifying.

He seized the glass as soon as offered and drained it; and then he turned to Alessandra. 'You've got some explaining to do,' he said.

The tears were very near the surface now.

She waited.

'How did you know it was Rosencranz?' he demanded. 'And the torpedoing – you knew about that. And don't think I've forgotten that we've met before – somewhere – don't worry, I'll think of where it was.'

She inclined her head, hiding her face.

'You're working for someone, aren't you?' Her silence was answer enough. 'A nice girl like you! How'd you get into this?' He shook his head, mystified.

'Ah, Meesta Gull,' she said brokenly, 'it's the old, old story. My 'usband – dead. My little ones – 'ungry. And what could I do? And now they 'ave me in their power.'

'Who?'

'The Black 'Ats, Meesta Gull. Yes, it is true. I am in the employ of your enemy.'

'But damn it, girl! I mean, you said you loved me!'

'I do! Truly! Oh, 'ow I do!'

'Now, wait a minute. You can't love *me* and work for *them,*' objected Gull.

'I can too! I do!'

'Prove it.'

She flared, ''Appily! 'Ow?'

Gull signalled for another drink. He smiled at the girl quite fondly. 'It's very simple,' he said. 'Just take me to your leader.'

7

It took a bit of doing, but the girl did it. She returned from a series of cryptic telephone conversations and looked at Gull with great, fearful eyes. 'I 'ave arranged it,' she said sombrely. 'You will be allowed in. But to get out again...'

Gull laughed and patted her hand. He was not worried.

Still, he admitted to himself a little later, things *could* get a bit difficult. Security precautions for the Black Hats were in no way less stringent than those of Gull's own headquarters in Marsport. He allowed himself to be seated in a reclining chair while a gnome-like old dentist drilled a totally unneeded filling into a previously healthy tooth; and when he rose, the exit through which he left the office brought him to a long, dark tunnel underground.

The girl was waiting there silently to conduct him to his destination. She placed a finger across her lips and led him away. 'Wait a minute,' Gull whispered fiercely, looking about. For there were interesting things here. Off the corridor were smaller chambers and secondary tunnels filled with all sorts of objects shadowy and objects small. Gull wanted very much to get a look at them. Those tiny disjointed doll-shapes! What were they? And the great gleaming disc section beyond?

But the girl was pleading, and Gull allowed himself to be led away.

She conducted him to a door. 'Be careful,' she whispered. And she was gone, and Gull was face to face with the chief of the Black Hats in Heliopolis.

He was a tall, saturnine man. He sat at a desk that reflected gold and green lights into his face, from signals that Gull could not see. 'Oodgay eveningway,' he said urbanely.

'Ah, I see you are perplexed. Perhaps you do not speak Solex Mal.'

'Afraid not. English, French, Cretan Linear B, Old Ganymedan's about the lot.'

'No matter. I am familiar with your tongue as we speak it all the time on Clarion.' He leaned forward suddenly. Gull stiffened; but it was only to hand him a calling card. It glittered with evil silver fires, and it read:

T. Perlman
Clarion

'Clarion's a planet? I've never heard of it.'

Perlman shrugged. Obviously what Gull had heard of did not matter. He said, 'You are a troublemaker, Mr Gull. We space people do not tolerate troublemakers for long.'

'As to that,' said Gull, stroking his goatee, 'it seems to me you had a couple of shots at doing something about it. And I'm still here.'

'Oh, no, Mr Gull,' said Perlman earnestly. 'Those were only warnings. Their purpose was only to point out to you that it is not advisable to cause us any trouble. You have not as yet done so, of course. If you do—' He smiled.

'You don't scare me.'

'No, Mr Gull?'

'Well, I mean, not much anyway. I've been lots more scared than this.'

'How interesting,' Perlman said politely.

'And anyway, I have my job to do and I'm going to do it.'

Perlman pursed his lips and whispered into a microphone on his desk. There was a stirring of draperies at the back of the room. It was shadowed there; Gull could see no details.

But he had a moment's impression of a face looking out at him, a great, sad, mindless long face with teeth like a horse and an air of infinite menace; and then it was gone. He cried, 'You're up to some trick!'

Perlman smirked knowingly.

'It won't do you any good! You think you know so much.'

'Ah, if only I did, Mr Gull! There are forces in this universe which even we of Clarion have not yet understood. The straightline mystery, to name one. The Father's plan.'

Gull took a deep breath and carefully, inconspicuously, released it. He was doing no good here. And meanwhile there were matters just outside this room that urgently required investigation – and attention. He said steadily, 'I'm going to go now, Mr Perlman. If you try to stop me I'll shoot you.'

Perlman looked at him with an expression that suspended judgement for a moment. Then it came to a conclusion and broke into a shout of laughter. 'Ho!' he choked. 'Hah! Oh, Mr Gull, how delicious to think you will be allowed to leave. As we say in Solex Mal, otway ustcray!'

Gull did not answer. He merely moved slightly, and into his hand leaped the concealed 3.15-picometre heat gun.

Perlman's expression changed from fire to ice.

'I'll leave you now,' said Gull. 'Next time you have a visitor, search his goatee too, won't you?'

Ice were Perlman's eyes. Icy was the stare that followed Gull out of the door.

But he was not safe yet, not while the horse-faced killer was presumably lurking somewhere about. The girl appeared silently and put her hand in his.

Gull gestured silence and strained his hearing. These tunnels were so dark; there were so many cul-de-sacs where an assassin could hide...

'Listen,' he hissed. 'Hear it? There!'

From the shadows, distant but approaching, came the sound of an uneven step. Tap, *clop*. Tap, *clop*.

The girl frowned. 'A man with one leg?' she guessed.

'No, no!' Can't you recognize it? It's a normal man – *but with one shoe hanging loose.*'

She caught her breath. 'Oh!'

'That's right,' said Gull sombrely, 'the old shoelace trick.

And I haven't time to deal with him now. Can you draw him off?'

She said steadily, 'If I 'ave to, I can.'

'Good. Just give me five minutes. I want to look around and – effect some changes, I think.' He listened, the step was closer now. He whispered, 'Tall, long-faced man with big teeth. I think that's him. Know him?'

'Certainly, dear Meesta Gull. Clarence T. Reik. 'E's a killer.'

Gull grinned tautly; he had thought as much. The partner of Harry Rosencranz, of course; one had attacked him at the hotel, the other was stalking him with a sharpened shoelace in the warrens under the city. 'Go along with you then,' he ordered. 'There's a good girl. Remember, five minutes.'

He felt the quick brush of her lips against his cheek. 'Give me 'alf a minute,' she said. 'Then, dear Meesta Gull, *run*.'

And she sprang one way, he another. The approaching tap, *clop* paused a split-second's hesitation.

Then it was going after her, its tempo rapid now, its sound as deadly as the irritable rattle of a basking snake.

Gull had his five minutes. He only prayed that it had not been bought at a higher price than he wanted to pay.

There in the Black Hat warrens under Heliopolis Johan Gull fulfilled the trust .5 placed in him. He had only moments. Moments would be enough. For almost at once he knew. And he leaned against the nitred stone walls of the catacomb, marvelling at the depth and daring of the Black Hat plan. Before him a chamber of headless, limbless mannikins awaited programming and assembly. They were green and tiny. In another chamber six flying saucers stood in proud array. Each of them held a ring of leather-cushioned seats. Behind him was a vast hall where signpainters had left their handiwork for the moment: *Read the OAHSPE Bible,* cried one sign; *Five Minutes for* $5. And another clamoured, *Welcome to UFOland.*

Gull nodded in unwilling tribute. The Black Hats had planned well...

A sound of light, running footsteps brought him back to reality. The pale shadow of the girl raced towards him. 'Well done!' he whispered, urging her on. 'Just one more time around and I'll be through.'

'It's 'ot work, dear Meesta Gull,' she laughed; but she obeyed. He froze until she was out of sight, and the lumbering dark figure that followed her. And then he set to work.

When she came by again he was ready.

Quickly he leaped to the centre of the corridor, gestured her to safety. She concealed herself in a doorway, panting, her eyes large but unafraid. And the pounding, deadly sound of her pursuer grew louder.

Fourteen semester hours of karate, a seminar in *le savate* and a pair of brass knuckles. All came to the aid of Johan Gull in that moment, and he had need of them. He propelled himself out of the shadows feet first, directly into the belly of the huge, long-faced man who was shambling down the dimly lit corridor. The man's eyes were dull but his great yellowed teeth were bared in a grin as he moved ferally along the stone floor, a thin, lethal wand in one hand, dangerous, ready.

Ready for a fleeing victim. Not ready for Johann Gull.

For Gull came in under the deadly needle. Even as he was plunging into the man's solar plexus he was reaching up with one hand, twisting around with the other. It was no contest. Gull broke the weapon-bearing arm between wrist and elbow, butted the man into paralysis, kicked him in the skull as he fell, snatched the weapon and was away, the girl trailing behind him.

'Hurry!' he called. 'If he comes to, they'll box us in here!' As he ran he worked one tip of the stiffened shoelace. Ingenious! Twisted one way, it slipped into limpness; twisted the other, it extended itself to become a deadly weapon. Gull chuckled and cast it away. Up the stairs they ran and through the cover dentist's office. The gnome-like dentist squalled in surprise and ran at them with a carbide drill, hissing hatred; but Gull chopped him down with the flat of a hand. They were free.

And the final battle was about to be fought.

8

'You 'ave a plan, Meesta Gull?'

'Of course.' He glanced about warily. No Black Hats were in sight as he led her through the bright, opulent doors of the Heliopolis Casino.

'You are going to fight them single-'anded?'

'Fight? My dear girl! Who said anything about fighting?' The *chef de chambre* was bowing, smiling, welcoming them in.

'But – But – But if you do not fight them, dear Meesta Gul, then 'ow will you proceed?'

Gull grinned tautly and led her to the bar, from which he could observe everything that was going on. He said only, 'Money. No more questions now, there's a good girl.'

He called for wine and glanced warily about. The Casino was host that night, as it was every night, to a gay and glittering crowd. Behind potted lichens a string trio sawed away at Boccherini and Bach, while the wealthiest and most fashionable of nine planets strolled and laughed and gamed away fortunes. Gull sipped his wine and stroked his goatee, his eyes alert. Now, if he had gauged his man aright – if he had assessed the strategy that would win correctly...

It could all be very easy, he thought, pleased. And he could enjoy a very pleasant half-hour's entertainment into the bargain.

Gull smiled and stroked the girl's hand. She responded with a swift look of trust and love. In the glowing silky fabric of the dress he had commandeered for her she was a tasty morsel, he thought. Once this Black Hat ploy had been countered, there might be time for more lighthearted pursuits...

'Attend!' she whispered sharply.

Gull turned slowly. So near his elbow as to be almost touching stood the tall, saturnine figure of Perlman. They stood for a moment in a tension of locked energies, eyes gazing into eyes. Then Perlman nodded urbanely and turned away. Gull heard him whisper to a passing houseman, 'Atthay's the erkjay.'

Gull leaned to the girl. 'I don't speak Solex Mal,' he said softly. 'You'll have to translate for me.'

She replied faithfully, ' 'E just identified you to the 'ouseman.'

He gave her an imperceptible nod and followed Perlman with his eyes. The Black Hat did not look towards Gull again. Smiling, exchanging a word now and then with the other guests, he was moving steadily towards the gaming tables. Gull allowed himself to draw one deep breath of satisfaction.

Score one for his deduction! Perlman was going to play.

He nodded to the girl and began to drift towards the tables himself. Give it time, he counselled himself. There's no hurry. Let it build. You were right this far, you'll be right again.

'Believe I'll play a bit,' he said loudly. 'Won't you sit here and watch, my dear?'

Silently the girl took a seat beside him at the table. Casually – but feeling, and relishing, the cold gambling tinge that spread upward from the pit in his stomach, inflaming his nerves, speeding the flow of his blood in his veins – Gull gestured to the croupier and began to play.

He did not look across the table at the polite assured face of Perlman. He did not need to. This game had only two players – or only two that mattered. As he took the dice for his first turn, Gull reflected with comfort and satisfaction that soon there would be only one.

Half an hour later he was all but broke.

Across the table Perlman's expression had broadened from polite interest, through amusement, to downright contempt. Gull's own face wore a frown; his hands shook, angering him; he felt the first cold prickling of fear.

Confound the man, thought Gull, his luck is fantastic! If indeed it was luck. But no, he told himself angrily, he could not cop out so cosily; the tables were honest. Face truth: he had simply run up against a superb gambler.

'Hell of a time for it to happen,' he grumbled.

The girl leaned closer. 'Pardon? You spoke?'

'No, no,' Gull said irritably, 'I – uh, was just thinking out loud. Listen. You got any money on you?'

She said doubtfully, 'Perhaps – a little bit...'

'Give it to me,' he demanded. 'No! Under the table. I don't want everybody to see.' But it was too late; across the table Perlman had not missed the little byplay. He was almost laughing openly now as he completed his turn and passed the dice to Gull.

Gull felt himself breathing hard. He accepted the thin sheaf of bills from the girl, glanced at it quickly. Not much! Not much at all for what he had to do. He could stretch it out, make it last – but for how long? And with the game running against him...

Silently Gull cursed and studied the table. Before him the wealth of an empire was piled in diamond chips and ruby, in pucks of glittering emeralds and discs of glowing gold.

Politely the croupier said, 'It is your play, m'sieur.'

'Sure, sure.' But still Gull hesitated. To gain time he tossed the girl's wad down before the croupier and demanded it to be exchanged for chips.

Across the table Perlman's look was no longer either amusement or contempt. It was triumph.

Gull took a deep breath. This was more than a game, he reminded himself. It was the careful carrying out of a thoughtfully conceived strategy. Had he lost sight of that?

Once again in control of himself, he took out a cigarette and lit it. He tipped the gleaming, flat lighter and glanced, as though bored, at its polished side.

Tiny in the reflection he could see the moving, bright figures in the room, the gorgeously dressed women, the distinguished men. But some were not so distinguished. Some were lurking in the draperies, behind the potted lichens. A great pale creature with teeth like a horse, eyes like a dim-brained cat. Another with the mahogany face of a prospector off the Martian plains. And others.

Perlman's men had come to join him. The moment was ready for the taking.

Abruptly Johan Gull grinned. Risk it all! Win or lose! Let the game decide the victor – either he would clean out Perlman here and now, and starve out his larger game for lack of the cash to carry it through, or he himself would lose. He said to the croupier, 'Keep the chips. Take these too.' And he pushed over all his slim remaining stack.

'You wish to build, m'sieur?' it asked politely.

'Exactly. A hotel, if you please. On the' – Gull hesitated, but not out of doubt; his pause was only to observe the effect on Perlman – 'yes, that's right. On the Boardwalk.'

And Gull threw the dice.

Time froze for him. It was not a frightening thing; he was calm, confident, at ease. The world of events and sensation seemed to offer itself to him for the tasting – the distant shout of the UFO demonstrators in the streets – *poor fools! I wonder what they'll do when they find they've been duped*; Alessandra's perfumed breath tickling his ear – *sweet, charming girl*; the look of threat and anger on Perlman's face; the stir of ominous movement in the draperies. Gull absorbed and accepted all of it, the sounds and scents, the bright moving figures and the glitter of wealth and power, the hope of victory and the risks. But he did not fear the risks. He saw Ventnor Avenue and Marvin Gardens looming ahead of his piece on the board and smiled. He was certain the dice were with him.

And when the spots came up he seemed hardly to glance at them; he moved his counter with a steady hand, four, five, eight places; came to rest on 'Chance', selected a card from the stack, turned it over and scanned its message.

He looked up into the hating eyes of Perlman. 'Imagine,'

he breathed. 'I appear to have won second prize in a beauty contest. You'll have to give me fifteen dollars.'

And Perlman's poise broke. Snarling, he pushed across the chips, snatched the dice from Gull and contemptuously flung them down. The glittering cubes rattled and spun. Gull did not have to look at the board; the position was engraved on his brain. A five would put Perlman on Park Place, with four houses: damaging, but not deadly. An eight or higher would carry him safely to 'Go' and beyond, passing the zone of danger and replenishing his bankroll. But a seven... Ah, a seven! The Boardwalk, with a hotel! And the first dice had already come to rest, displaying a four.

The second stopped.

There was a gasp from the glittering crowd as three bright pips turned upward to the light.

Gull glanced down at the dice, then across at Perlman. 'How unfortunate,' he murmured politely, extended a hand to Perlman – and only Perlman could see the bright, deadly little muzzle that pointed out of it towards him. 'You seem to have landed on my propery. I'm afraid you've lost the game.'

And he was up and out of his chair, standing clear, as the pencil of flame from the shelter of the draperies bit through the smoky air where his head had just been.

'Down!' he shouted to the girl and snapped a shot at Rosencranz; heard that man's bellow of pain and saw, out of the corner of his eye, that the girl had disobeyed his order; she had drawn a weapon of her own and was trading shot for shot with the Black Hats that ringed the room. 'Idiot!' Gull cried, but his heart exulted *Good Girl!* even as he was turning to blast the next Black Hat. There were nine of them, all armed all drawing their weapons or, like Rosencranz, having fired them already. It was not an equal contest. Five shots from Gull, five from the girl – she missed one – and all the Black Hats were on the floor, writhing or very still. All but one. Perlman! Whirling back to face him, Gull found he was gone.

But he couldn't be far. Gull caught the flicker of motion in the gaping crowd at the door that showed where he had gone, and followed. At the entrance Gull caught a glimpse of him and fired; at the corner, plunging through a knot of milling, excited UFOlogist, Gull saw him again – almost too late. Coolly and cleverly Perlman had waited him out, his own weapon drawn now. The blast sliced across the side of Gull's head like a blow from a cleaver; stunned, hurting, Gull drove himself on.

And as Perlman, gaping increduously, turned belatedly to flee again, he tripped and stumbled, and Gull was on him. His head was roaring, his hold on consciousness precarious; but he pinned Perlman's arms in a desperate flurry of strength and panted, 'That's enough! Give it up or I'll burn your head off.' The trapped man surged up but Gull withstood it and cried: 'Stop! I want to take you back to .5 alive – don't make me kill you!' The Black Hat spat one angry sentence; Gull gasped and recoiled; Perlman grabbed for the weapon, they struggled ...

A bright line of flame leapt from the gun to Perlman's forehead; and, in that moment the leader of the Black Hats in Heliopolis ceased to be.

Waves of blackness swept over Johan Gull. He fell back into emptiness just as the girl came running up, dropped to the ground beside him, sobbing, 'Johan! My dear, *dear* Meesta Gull.'

Hurt and almost out he managed to grin up at her. 'Cash in my chips for me,' he gasped. 'We've won the game!'

9

And then it was roses, roses all the way. The local Bureau Chief appeared and efficiently arranged for medical attention, fresh clothes and a drink. The girl stayed beside him while Gull dictated a report and demanded immediate reservations back to Marsport – for *two*, he specified fiercely. They were produced, and by the time they disembarked and headed for the War Room, Gull was nearly his old self.

He was admitted at once to .5's office, and recognized it as a mark of signal favour when the girl was allowed in with him.

They stood there, proud and silent, in the presence of .5 and his secretary, and Gull's hand was firm on the girl's. What a thoroughbred she was, he thought admiringly, noting from the corner of his eye how her gaze took in every feature of the room so few persons had ever seen; how she studied .5's sombre expression and hooded eyes, but did not quail before them; how patiently and confidently she waited for McIntyre to leave off writing in his notebook and speak to them. She would be a fit wife for him, thought Johan Gull with quiet certainty; and she would make a fine agent for Security. And so would Kim, and Marie Celeste, and little Patty. A very successful mission all round, thought Gull cheerfully, thinking of the wad of bills that Perlman's losses had put into his wallet.

'When you're quite ready, Gull,' said McIntyre.

Gull jumped. 'Oh, sorry,' he said. 'Excuse me, sir,' he added to .5, whose expression showed no particular resentment at being kept waiting while one of his agents was woolgathering, merely the usual patient weariness. 'I guess you want a report.'

'.5 has already seen your report,' McIntyre reproved him. 'He is a little concerned about your failure to obey standing orders, of course. A live captive is worth a lot more than a dead loser.'

'Well, yes, I know that's right. But—' Gull hesitated.

'Well?'

Gull flushed and turned to .5 himself. 'You see, sir, it was something Perlman *said*. Nasty sort of remark. Cheap. Just what you'd expect, from – anyway, sir, it was about you. He said—' Gull swallowed, feeling self-conscious and stupid. The warm pressure of the girl's hand showed him her sympathy, but he still felt like twelve kinds of a fool bringing it up.

'Gull! Spit it out before .5 loses his patience!'

Gull shrugged, looked his chief in the eye and said

rapidly, 'Perlman said you've been dead since '97, sir.' And he waited for the blow to fall.

Surprisingly, it did not. .5 merely continued to look at him, silently, levelly, appraisingly. There was not even a hint of surprise in his expression. At length McIntyre laughed one sharp, desiccated sort of laugh and Gull turned gratefully towards him, glad to be taken off the hook. 'Nonsense, of course, McIntyre,' he said. 'I really hated to have to say it.'

But McIntyre was raising a hand, chuckling in a sort of painful way, as though laughter hurt him. 'Never mind, Gull. After all, you're not expected to evaluate information. Just go on and do your job. And now, .5 had best be left alone for a while; there are other matters concerning us, you know.'

And, very grateful to have it happen, Gull found himself and the girl outside. He discovered he was sweating. 'Whew,' he exclaimed. 'Wouldn't want to go through *that* again. And now, my dear, I suggest a drink – thereafter a wedding – then a honeymoon. Not necessarily in that order.'

'Gladly, dearest Meesta Gull!' she cried. 'And I don't give a 'ang about the order!'

Science Fiction in Pan

Bob Shaw
THE PALACE OF ETERNITY 30p

John Boyd
THE LAST STARSHIP FROM EARTH 30p

Kingsley Amis and Robert Conquest
SPECTRUM Volumes 1–5, each at 30p

Isaac Asimov
NINE TOMORROWS 30p

Edited by Damon Knight
100 YEARS OF SCIENCE FICTION Vol. I 30p
100 YEARS OF SCIENCE FICTION VOL. II 30p

Alfred Bester
THE DARK SIDE OF THE EARTH 25p

Arthur C. Clarke
A FALL OF MOONDUST 30p
THE DEEP RANGE 30p
EARTHLIGHT 25p
CHILDHOOD'S END 30p

Ray Bradbury
R IS FOR ROCKET 30p
S IS FOR SPACE 30p

C. S. Lewis
VOYAGE TO VENUS 30p
OUT OF THE SILENT PLANET 30p
THAT HIDEOUS STRENGTH 30p

Occult and Supernatural

Frank Edwards	
STRANGE PEOPLE	20p
Muriel Grey	
THE BOOK OF DREAMS	30p
Rosalind Heywood	
THE SIXTH SENSE	35p
THE INFINITIVE HIVE	35p
Douglas Hunt	
EXPLORING THE OCCULT	30p
June Johns	
KING OF THE WITCHES (illus)	25p
Eric Maple	
THE DARK WORLD OF WITCHES (illus)	30p
THE REALM OF GHOSTS	30p
Leon Petulengro	
SECRETS OF ROMANY ASTROLOGY AND PALMISTRY	20p

Ira Levin

ROSEMARY'S BABY 25p

'At last I have got my wish. I am ridden by a book that plagues my mind and continues to squeeze my heart with fingers of bone. I swear that Rosemary's Baby is the most unnerving story I've read' – KENNETH ALLSOP

'. . . . if you read this book in the dead of night, do not be surprised if you feel the urge to keep glancing behind you' – QUEEN

'a darkly brilliant tale of modern deviltry that like James' Turn of the Screw, induces the reader to believe the unbelievable. I believed it and was altogether enthralled'

– TRUMAN CAPOTE

A KISS BEFORE DYING 25p

THIS PERFECT DAY 35p

Ghost & Horror in Pan